Here Sat
A Key Maker...

of Friendship, Love, Hate and Men.

Here Sat
A Key Maker...

of Friendship, Love, Hate and Men.

Dr. Makarand Lohire

Srishti
PUBLISHERS & DISTRIBUTORS

Srishti Publishers & Distributors
N-16, C. R. Park
New Delhi 110 019
srishtipublishers@gmail.com

First published by Srishti Publishers & Distributors in 2013
Copyright © Dr. Makarand Lohire, 2013

ALL MAJOR CHARACTERS IN THIS NOVEL ARE 100% FICTITIOUS ANY
RESEMBLANCE TO ANYONE LIVING, DEAD OR TO BE BORN IS PURELY
COINCIDENTAL

Typeset in AGaramond 12pt. by Suresh Kumar Sharma at Srishti

Contents

Acknowledgements

There are many to whom I would like to thank for making my dream come true.

This book wouldn't have been possible without the blessings of God, who scripted various instances in my life, so that I can use them on the name of fiction.

Thanks to my parents and brothers, who encouraged me to continue writing and boosted my confidence by their comments for my write-ups.

Thanks to my friend Dr. Dipen Walvatkar whose editing and valuable suggestions made wonders with the write-up. Throughout the process of writing, he had been most helpful and I really thank him for keeping his cool while reading the initial draft in my bad handwriting. Also, thanks to Hari Iyer and Raksheet Shetty for helping out with the editing and for their helpful comments.

Thanks to Dr. Deepak Pokra and Mahi MK for helping with the cover page design. I know my silly questions must have frustrated you during the process, but I am sure you can understand how keen I was.

Also, many thanks to Rahul, Mahesh, Priety, Shikha, Tirath, Unzer, Muni, Avinash, Raskar, Asha, Duaa and Vicky for letting me use their names in the story. Though I know, some of them might be cursing me for that, but guys, I am sorry for that, and you know how much I mean that. Thanks to Debanshu for being my inspiration, as you might not know, but it was your short story which made me start writing. I am grateful to my other friends as well for reading the manuscript and helping me with their comments.

Thanks to Dinesh *mama,* for sharing the instances during family gatherings, which he had seen or heard, which were real or fictional, I don't know, but that surely helped me a lot.

Thanks to Srishti publishers, who helped and guided me in a brilliant way to make the book even better. I am really thankful to them for believing in my work and supporting me.

I am also obliged to Grant medical college, Mumbai, which gave me an identity as a GMCite and trained me to believe in myself.

And last but not the least, thanks to 'Dr. Bhatia Classes' notepad, which they distribute outside the exam centre, because those are the ones in which I wrote the manuscript.

Prologue

Last night was hell! I mean, you don't encounter seriously ill patients every other minute every night. It was my turn for emergency duty and for the entire night, I was busy pushing gelcos and doing blood collections; after all that is what an intern is destined to do. Finally in the wee hours of the morning, I was just about to collapse for want of some sleep and was looking forward to some rest in the side room; I had to make do with an old chair in the emergency ward. I was the lone medicine intern that night and my senior wouldn't allow me any rest in the side room. A doctor's life is full of emergencies, something I didn't like at all, because sleep is something which is most precious to me.

Walking past the CT scan centre of J.J Hospital, I got a call from my senior. "Makarand, where are you right now?" he growled in his frustrated, angry, grumpy tone.

I wanted to reply with the perfect words for him, but I controlled myself, thinking about his completion signature on my journal which was the lone reason why I had to put up with his nonsense.

"Sir, I was leaving for the hostel."

Senior, "Did you complete all the blood collections for last night's patients? If not, I want it to be done stat."

'Stat' is the most static word in every medico's language.

I usually did all the work before leaving. But, that morning, I was too tired to finish all blood collections. So, I had left a couple of them. "Yes sir, it's all done," I lied, and then ending the call, I quickly switched off my cell phone.

Walking past the Pediatrics ward, dragging myself, struggling to defy gravity, I finally reached 'Apna' boys hostel. 'Apna' boy's hostel is the most drab hostel, one could find. I walked up the steps to reach out for the lift. Leaning on the sidewall, I pressed the button to call the lift. No effect....no sound.

I pressed it twice. Still no movement of the lift wires.

That was the usual scene here. So, I started walking up the stairs. My room was on the 4th floor..room no. 145. It was hard for me to keep awake. So, counting the floors, finally I reached my room.

I was eager to get to my bed and feel the state of oblivion. But as I reached my room, I saw that the room was locked. My roommates, Rahul and Raskar, usually stayed at home. Raskar had his own key that he kept with his all other personal keys, but Rahul and I shared the same key that we used to keep on the ventilator.

So, I extended my hand to the ventilator, feeling for the key. With tired closed eyes, tapping softly over the ventilator's muddy floor, for an onlooker it would look as if I was reading some Braille script. When I couldn't find the key I tried looking for it stretching my neck and toes.

To my horror, there was no key there. I quickly switched on my mobile and phoned Rahul, "*Abey*, where are you? The key isn't on the venti."

Rahul, in his sleepy language, "*Arey*, I had kept it there...ask Raskar, he was there yesterday."

I called Raskar, "Raskar, did you take the key from venti..where are you?"

Raskar, "*Arey yaar*, I am sorry. I am at home and I had brought your key with me, by mistake."

Listening to those words, anyone would make him recollect his ancestors. But, I kept silent, cut the call and switched off my mobile. I kept my cool because I knew him; such behaviour was usual on his part.

After thinking for other ways to get in, I inferred it would be better to go to the roadside key-maker, to get a duplicate one made.

It was close to 9 in the morning already and the roadside shops had opened up and there was the usual hustle bustle. Quickly I rushed to the corner on the footpath next to our hostel gate, where a young key-maker used to sit. There was no one there. So I started walking further in search of some key-maker.

But that day, I wasn't able to get one. Walking by, I saw a store of locks and keys. Though I thought, it would be absurd to ask for a key-maker at such a big store, being in need, I stepped inside and asked a young boy there, "Hey, I want someone to come with me to make a key for a lock; I have lost the original."

He stared at me for a moment.

"Oh..actually, I am a doctor. I stay at Apna boy's hostel." I said.

He smiled, "Ya..ya. I was just checking out your not so clean apron. Sirji, try to get it washed, sometime."

I was so tired that I forgot to remove my apron. So I quickly did that. Then, he told somebody to look after his store and came with me.

We both were silent till we arrived at the hostel gate. To break the silence, I said to him, "There used to be a key maker on that footpath, some months back. But, he wasn't there. That's why I had to walk till I reached your store."

He laughed and asked, "Sirji, don't you remember his face?"

Me "No… why?"

He said, "Sirji, I am the same boy."

I was surprised to hear that, "Wow! Great. From a mere stall to a store, and that too in just few months, what's the secret *haan*?"

Suddenly he became silent and walked up to my room, tongue-tied.

Finally, don't know why, but he asked, "Sirji, I will tell you the story behind my success, but promise you won't tell it to anybody."

I said, "Sure."

With an anxious voice, he said, "Actually, I always wanted to tell somebody this and you seem to be a nice fellow, are you willing to listen?"

And then for the next two hours, he narrated his story. I got so engrossed in it that I forgot my sleep.

So I would be telling you the story of this key-maker, Javed from his point of view, as well from the outlook of Sashank, the other character of this story.

1

JAVED'S LIFE

'Shit! What's happening *yaar*. My hands had started hurting now. I had been chipping away at this godforsaken piece of metal for a good 30-40 minutes, but this rotten lock was betraying me today.

On top of that, the thing that was irritating me most was this elderly Parsi uncle who was standing besides me all this while and scrutinizing my work. He was a typical *bawa*, in his late 70s, dressed in a plain white, somewhat transparent *kurta pajama* with that signature cap on his head. He had been standing next to me from the moment I entered his house, though he never uttered a word, I could sense his disapproval each time I tried the key in the lock unsuccessfully as he let out a long sigh. The sighs were coming more and more frequently now. He mirrored my expressions each time I looked at him. When I smiled at him, he smiled back, when I looked at him with a helpless face, he regarded me with the same emotion.

Insha Allah, let this try be a success. *Hatt*..failed again. My brain had stopped working. The dingy little room and the ever so slowly moving fan weren't helping either; I preferred working in the open and was progressively getting frustrated without much success. I was seriously beginning to doubt my skill now. Sitting there, disappointed with the tools in my hand, I felt like offering money to my client and telling him to buy a new suitcase.

But, where do I get the money from? These days, I was in desperate need of money. The suitcase and the Parsi gentleman were both testing my patience with a blank response. Renewing my resolve, I worked on the lock for few more minutes. But the words had begun to loom large at the back of my mind, "Now, it needs to be broken."

I was about to cede, when I heard the sweet noise… Click! It was like music to my ears, at last the lock had opened. I heaved a sigh of relief.

"Here's your key, uncle. It really took a lot of effort to make it. It would be better if you make a duplicate of it right now, else you might be in trouble if this one is misplaced."

Uncle "*Nahin re dikra*. There's no need for it. First let me check if this key works properly or not."

The man then proceeded to open and close the suitcase with the key repeatedly for about 15-20 times in front of me and asked "So, how much for this small key?"

I didn't know what to say, the old man didn't look like he could afford to pay me 200 Rs, which I usually charged for home visits. So I told him, "*Chalo* uncle, give me what you feel like."

Then uncle took out a 50 rupee note from his half-torn pocket and smilingly said, "*Chal haan dikra*. Next time if I need to get a key made, I will call u and will also suggest your name to others."

The man promised me future contracts - something that I was desperately in need of. So, without uttering a word, I accepted the note.

Then I took out my entry book and handed it to uncle "Take this, write your name, address, the bag for which the key was made, and sign next to it."

Uncle "Why *re*?"

I always disliked this part of my job, explaining clients the reason for signing in the record book, the heading itself was self explanatory. 'Record book' was written in large letters on the cover page. So, once again cooling down my frustration, I explained it to him, "We, key-makers have to keep a record of the work done. The police people check it."

Giving a nod with raised eyebrows, indicating that he understood the point, he started searching for a pen. After rummaging in every drawer of his ancient showcase, finally he got one. Then he wrote the details in the book, slowly with his trembling hand.

As soon as he inked the final dot after his tremulous signature, I moved out.

I was very hungry, it was almost 4 in the evening and I hadn't had anything since morning. As I left the Parsi *bawa's* old building, I started looking around for some place to eat. Having some money in my pocket had increased my hunger somewhat. Just then I came across a *vada pav* stall.

Vada pav is the most common fast food in Mumbai. It satisfies your hunger instantly for just six rupees. The sight of the hot *vadas* and the smell of freshly cut onions and *chutney* was difficult to resist, my mouth had already started watering. I quickly ordered a *vada pav*. It was good; I loved the red chutney and freshly cut onion mixture that the stall owner had stuffed into the *pav*. I had my fill and rinsed my mouth with the water kept in a *lota* beside the stall.

Suddenly, I realised that it was the time to regard my *Allah*. I quickly ran from there to my special seat at the traffic signal next to J.J Hospital. It was peak hour and the streets were crowded, but I had my place reserved. So what if it was just a roadside stone, for me, it was like a throne.

I made myself comfortable on the stone with minor adjustments. Perched on my throne, I could look at each and every passing commuter, at the signal. But, luck wasn't favoring me today. As time moved on, my hopes were getting fainter. Though I waited for an hour, she didn't come. Disappointed, I decided to move on and headed towards my humble abode. It was a 4 feet by 6 feet piece of footpath which I had inherited from *chacha*. Going by the current rate, this piece of the municipal footpath could cost anything between 3 to 4 lakh rupees, but I could sleep there at 10 rupees per day, thanks to the *topiwala mamu*.

The place was next to the back gate of J.J Hospital and a few meters away from the local unofficial garbage dump. It was nothing to be proud of but I was thankful to *Allah* for whatever I had. I had been through much worse times than today.

I grew up in a small orphanage in Umer khadi. My parents had left me there when I was a few days old. The *aaya* took pity on me and raised me. However I was very weak in my childhood as she couldn't afford to spend too much money on me, there were many mouths to feed. However, I recovered, but was bullied all the time by the bigger, stronger boys. Not only I, but almost all the younger kids were fed up of them, except some who preferred to be their *chamchas*. But still, their main targets were my friend, chintu and I. He was a cute looking boy, quite well mannered. We got along well and spent most of our time in each others company. We used to hide together when the bullies came for ragging us and we also shared our food. Luckily he was saved from this when we were in 2nd standard, as he was adopted by some couple. His cute looks helped him to be so lucky. That day both of us cried a lot. I never saw him again. I felt disheartened as he was my only companion in the orphanage.

We had a small school in our orphanage where people would come to teach us gratis. I studied there till the 4th standard. By the time I was 8 years old, the orphanage ran into some financial difficulties; as a result it became impossible for the *aaya* to look after all the inmates. There was fighting for food and as a result I went hungry most of the time. Finally one day I decided to take matters in my own hands. I left the orphanage, even though I knew of no other place where I could get shelter. I begged people for jobs, but never for money. A *sardarji* took pity on me and gave me a job in his hotel. I worked there for two years, it was a small place but I enjoyed the work. Importantly, I had food and shelter. However, it was not to last long. One fine day, the manager falsely accused me of stealing money from the counter. I was beaten by my fellow waiters and thrown out. I was on the streets again. Those few months were really bad.

Finally, I got work at a local *chai tapri*, the owner was a good fellow and I was happy to work with him. Even though my salary was a meagre Rs 300, but I got *chai nasta* free every day. While at the *tapri*, I met *chacha*. He was an old fellow, who made keys for a living and I found that fascinating.

Over a period of time, we developed a fine rapport. He used to take me to the mosque regularly and instilled good values in me. He also taught me preachings of the Quran. After working at the *tapri* for almost a year, *chacha* took me with him and I went along happily. Over the next year, I learnt the art of making keys from him. He was like a father to me and loved me a lot as he too was alone in this world. We lived our modest life on this very footpath and this was the very place where he was crushed to death by a speeding vehicle in the dead silence of the night four years back. He was taken away by the police and cremated. The owner of the car was never found. I was shattered by his loss and cried for days, but then I remembered his words *"Tumne yeh fann seekh liya hai, mere baad bhi tum iske dam par apne pairo pe khade ho sakte ho."*

So I followed his advice and have been working with my old tools ever since on this roadside corner. Umer khadi has been my world since then.

Umer khadi is an old settlement near Sandhurst Rd. station in Mumbai, made famous by the J.J Hospital, which has been here for many years, serving the diseased and injured. It is a very crowded place, where you will find people from every religion, from every strata of society. Most of the buildings here have been here since the pre independence days, but a few skyscrapers have sprung up in the last few years. Still, this place retains its old world ambience. Many people stay in these old buildings, in spite of the government labelling them as - *"Dhokadayak imarat"*. What it actually meant was that the building could collapse at any point of time and that the authorities would not be responsible for any loss of lives or property.

You will find many contradicting instances here. Like the complex here named 'Amir building'. You can easily make out, just looking at the dilapidated building, how rich the residents might be. Whenever I walk near it, I fear that it would collapse on me; I wonder how people live in it. I guess the answer to my question is the same thing that is cemented on every person on this earth...*majboori.*

However, I am not alone in this world. I have a true friend, Chhamiyaan. He was also adopted by *chacha*, the only difference being that he was a dog. We have been friends for four years; he was just a puppy then. I was the one who had given him this weird name; it helped me to fill the void of a girlfriend in my life. Initially he didn't like this name, but as time passed he grew used to it. We share everything, eat the same food, and even share the same bed, our footpath.

Next day
Finally, my dream girl made an appearance. You know, for that one

moment, I forget every sorrow of my sleazy life; such is her magic. She looks so good.

She was on a scooty, dressed in blue jeans and a pink top. Her fair skin and long brown hair, made her look awesome, especially when she left her hair loose. She was about my height, the only thing we had in common. Her light brown eyes matched her hair. She was like a magnet and I was like a rusted piece of iron, attracted towards her.

Whenever she came at the signal, each and every *tharkeey* used to stare at her. I felt a strong desire to give a punch to those *tharkeeys*, but what to do; I am not that strong physically. Also, what was I to her? She had never looked at me in all these years, but I kept on hoping.

Three minutes....yes, that was the time for which the signal was closed. Then the signal turned green and there she zoomed out of my sight on her scooty. I didn't even know what she did, whether she was a student or working. I guessed that she studied in a college. She seemed to be a nice girl and was always dressed in simple yet fashionable attire; I like that. *Aakhir sundarta saadgi mein hoti hai...*Hrithik has said in Kaho na pyaar hai.

As soon as she was out of my sight, my eyes fell upon a 500 rupee note. However it soon went into a policeman's pocket and out of my sight. A police officer was accepting bribe. The person bribing him seemed to be a college boy. He was seated in a stylish white car and looked rich. *Saala*, the whole world cheats. And the worst thing is that the cheaters get away scotfree. Only the innocent people carry the burden of honesty, this world has no 500 rupess notes to offer to hard working, honest persons like me. Life has become rubbish.

Wrapping up the deal, the police officer walked towards me and said, "What Javed, how's everything…fine *na*."

He was the local constable, the hand of law who was always seen roaming, looking for his *chai paani*, anything from 50 to 500 rupees depending on the nature of the 'crime'. The culprits would most often be youngsters driving without a license or helmets. The bigger the vehicle, the larger the bribe. Then satisfied with his 'duty' he would reward himself with a *mawa paan* and get back to his job, spitting red mini missiles all over my footpath.

He knew me well and was somehow nice to me. Saluting him for showing the respect, though I didn't have any, I said, "Fine, *saab*."

He seemed happy, which was evident by the subdued smile on his face. But, still I was confused about the emotion as his face was camouflaged by the ultra-large moustache.

Then, I don't know why, he took out a bundle of hundred rupee notes from his right pocket, took a 50 rupee note from it, and said,

"Take this Javed, consider it as a treat from me, I am very happy today."

Money, that too from a police officer; one needs to be very lucky to experience that. However, my conscience defeated that too. I never took free cash from anybody; it was against my values.

"*Saab*, no…thank you. You know that I don't accept such money. Ya, if you have some work for me, then please tell me."

Police officer, "What work should I give you; my lock-up is full of talented thieves, who can prepare the keys faster than you."

It was true that thieves were far better than me, that's why they had the confidence to do the robberies.

The police officer stood there laughing with his belly wabbling with each gust. Suddenly, he slowed down and asked, "*Arey* Javed, there has been a theft at Kalbadevi; the locker was looted by opening its door. Do you have any information about it? Did you do any job, there?"

"No *saab*, I don't have any idea about that, I haven't done any work there. If you want, you can check my book."

Police officer "Oh Javed, I can make out a crook just by looking at him. I do not need to check your book. I trust your word."

Those words made me feel good. Though I doubted his honesty, then that's how life was in this city, even he must have a family to feed.

That night 11.45 pm

There were 35 Rs left from the previous day's earnings. I went to Shabbir *bhai's* stall to have some food. Shabbir *bhai* was famous for his omelettes, *bhurji* and *cutting*; light on the pocket and heavy on the stomach. That was why I would frequently go there. Cheap food always attracts people, not only me but many others like me would crowd his little *tapri* late in the evening. Many doctors and medical students from the neighbouring J.J Hospital would come there to eat, they could be easily recognised from their white coats. It was just in front of J.J Hospital casualty, and stayed open till late at night serving both doctors and patients alike. I ordered one single *bhurji pav* and stood there, hearing the conversation of two doctors, who were there having their late night meal.

1st doc, "*Abbey*, why are you attending the posting?"

2nd doc, "Why, what should I do then, the Chief knows me by name."

1st doc, "*Abbey*, just give 2000 to Naik. Any posting can be managed."

2nd doc, "What are you saying, Naik *khaata hai*! *Sahi hai*. I will certainly meet him tomorrow then."

Even people in this noble profession are not averse to bribing someone for their benefit, I thought to myself.

"*Yeh lo bhai.*" Shabbir bhai said.

"*Haan shukriya bhai…*"

I had my fill of the *bhurji pav*, cleared my throat with the hot tea and left for my footpath abode after paying him.

I heard some chaos as I was passing a roadside restaurant and bar. I stopped to see what the fuss was about. A boy was standing in front of the manager, leaning on the counter as if his legs were about to give in "*Arey uncle*, take as much money as you want, but give me one bottle of vodka. *Bas kya*"

I went a little closer and saw that it was the same guy who had bribed the policeman in the evening. He looked very drunk. Clumsily he took out a wad of 100 Rs notes and kept it in front of the bar manager, repeating the same words.

But the bar manager was reluctant "*Nai saab, abhi band karne ka time ho chuka hai..* the police would be coming for their rounds… *khaali phukat panga mat karo..*"

- "*Kuch nai hoga uncle, unko bhi khila denge thoda..*"

"*Bar band kiya hai sir… mai to hisab kar ne ke liye ruka tha…. Abhi nahi milega..*"

There were two other boys standing behind that boy and they looked similarly drunk but they were somehow trying to convince him to leave, but he was not even listening to them. The bar manager was adamant as it was already well past 12 pm and he didn't want to risk an altercation with the police at this hour.

Handling the situation well, his friends picked up the money and took him to sit in the car. Meanwhile, the *hawaldar* who was watching all this from a distance, finally sprang into action and started blowing his whistle as he walked towards the bar. Hearing that whistle, the boys quickly s

ped away in their car, while the bar manager quickly pulled down the shutter.

I realised in a matter of seconds that everyone had fled and the policeman was coming towards me, still blowing his whistle. I ran away.

2

JAVED
"HAPPY BIRTHDAY TO ME"

Night 1.05 am

"Happy birthday to you…hey..congrats *yaar. Tum jiyo hazaaron saal….cheerz…*"

I was sleeping peacefully with Chhamiyaan by my side, when I heard some commotion. Not wanting to open my eyes, I wondered to myself whether this was some kind of a dream. But as the din grew louder I could make out the words, and was further confused as I myself didn't know my birthday, so how could anyone else know it and come to celebrate it with me at this unearthly hour. Chhamiyaan had woken up too, and started barking near my ears. I held him by his ear and pulled him down to sit, but he wouldn't budge and went on barking. I had no other option but to wake up.

15

Sleepily I sat up and looked around me for the source of the noise. As my vision cleared, I saw some three or four people standing outside a car parked on the roadside, with beer bottles in their hands and plates of food on the bonnet of the car, cheering and celebrating what I suppose was their friend's birthday. It was then I realised that the voices were of these people. I sat at my place, watching them happily celebrate the moment.

Watching them, I felt both – a wave of happiness and sadness together. How lucky they were! They lived each and every moment of their life lavishly while I languished on this roadside corner. They strived to make their birthdays extra-special while I on the other hand didn't even know when mine was. There were very few moments in my life that I could cherish. Luck was one of the things that God had forgotten to pack in my bag. No wonder, I always struggled to survive. I didn't even know my birthday! But yes, I was surely born on some date in some year, so what if I was later dumped into an orphanage by my parents. Yeah, every person born on this earth has a date of birth. Even I wanted a reason to celebrate.

That very moment I decided to celebrate the next day as my birthday. At least I would try my best to do so.

Next day: morning,

Arey uth Javed. Abey uth. Girahik aayla hai." I woke up on hearing my name, I didn't recognise the voice at first but later I saw that it was Sonu, the roadside beggar. I got up. A boy who seemed to be in his teens was standing in front of me holding a key in his hand.

He said, "I want to get a duplicate made for this key. How much will it cost?"

I said, "Twenty rupees."

After arguing a bit on the cost, I did the work for eighteen rupees and then decided to have a bath before my morning namaaz. Luckily the tap of nearby Umer khadi chawl was not very crowded. So I didn't have to wait for long or push my way through. I bathed quickly, dusted my clothes and wore them again, smoothed down the few strands of hair that stood upright on my head, combed it with my fingers, wore my clean slippers and was off to the mosque in 10 minutes. At the mosque, I prayed *Allah* to forgive me for my sins and bless me as I would celebrate my birthday today. If my parents had been alive, I would have known my birthday.

My next stop was Nagori Snack Corner. This shop is famous all over Byculla for its cakes, tea, lassi and many other delicacies. I took a moment to look for the cake I wanted. In the display were kept numerous different slices of cake and pastries in rows, rectangular in shape in thin rectangular plastic containers with their price tags. Each one looked appetizing; I was confused never having had any of these before. Just then I noticed a beautiful piece kept on the top row. It was brown and white in alternate layers with a bright red cherry on top. The price tag read Rs. 15.

"Give me this cake... and a *chai*," I ordered.

The shop owner who was eyeing me suspiciously all this while took some time to realise which one I was ordering, then proceeded to pick up a piece of *mawa* cake that was kept below the one I wanted. I stopped him and said, "No, no, not this one, the one above it.."

"That is Dark Forest Pastry, not a slice of cake....and it is for Rs 15..*utna paisa hai kya??*"

I took out the 20 Rs note in great style and said "*Chalo abhi, time khoti mat karo.* I don't want to spoil my mood today."

Hearing my heavy dialogues, he stared at me for a few seconds and then ordered *chhotu* to take my order and went back to his chair. The owner was still staring at me. I too stared back at him for a moment. But then, I realised that I had to stay in this area for years with peace and knew that my conceit was momentary. So I gave him a smile and asked, "Please *chacha*, can you make it quick. The thing is that I am getting a little late. I will be really thankful to you if you bring my order quickly."

Some *mahapurush* has said that people behave with you, the way you behave with them. That day, I experienced that.

He replied, "*Haan saab*, just a minute. Oh, there comes *chhotu* with your pastry and *chai*."

The pastry looked very appealing. I didn't want the weariness I felt from standing to lessen my elated feeling of enjoying the cake, so I quickly took a corner seat on one of the already occupied benches and kept the *chai* on the table. I held the pastry and just enjoyed the soft feel of it in my hands. It was delicately done; the brown layer was actually made of numerous thin flakes of chocolate. I was almost drooling but controlled my urge to devour it at one go. I proceeded to eat it in small bites savouring every bite. The chocolate simply melted in my mouth and left a heavenly taste as it mingled with the cream. It was a great combination.

After enjoying the delicious pastry for a long time, I had the *chai*. It felt almost tasteless after the delicious pastry and I just gulped it down. I was lost in my modest meal for almost 15-20 minutes. After finishing it, I felt the urge to have another pastry. But I only had thirteen rupees, and I had to save money for lunch and dinner too. So, I got up, savouring the sweet aftertaste which was still lingering in my mouth.

The entire afternoon passed by without a single customer. I waited all the time hoping that someone might turn up saying, "I have lost my keys", or "I locked myself out of my house" or at least, "Make me a duplicate key". Somewhere in my mind there was a silent desire that someone would turn up and say, "Happy birthday Javed". But nobody was unlucky enough to come to me that afternoon. There go my birthday plans, I thought. I had already skipped lunch and by late afternoon, dinner was looking like a distant dream. Still, I waited.

Then, to make my birthday momentous, she arrived at the signal. The colours of our clothes were matching today. Both of us were in grey. It was a different matter that mine had turned into a dull shade of grey as they had not been washed for many days, she on the other hand was wearing a simple grey T-shirt with black jeans. She was wearing no make up today, no earrings as well. To me, she was looking even more beautiful without any make up. She had not put *kajal* in her eyes this time. As if she had somehow read my mind yesterday.....*sundarta saadgi me hoti hai.*

I had my eyes on her all the time, she was busy searching for something in her bag, then she took some papers out of it and started looking into them. Meanwhile, her bag was dangling by her side and a small purse fell out of it onto the road. She didn't notice it and went on sifting through the papers. No one else had noticed it either. There was still a minute for the signal to go green. I was getting tense with each passing second, 30 seconds to go... still she had no idea that her purse had fallen, she seemed preoccupied with something. The purse was lying quite near to where I was sitting. Mustering some courage I got up, quickly picked up the fallen purse, approached her and held the purse in front of her, with my hands trembling.. *"Madam..aa..aaa. aa aapka yeh pu..purse gir gaya tha."*

She quickly put aside her papers and snatched the purse from my hands, as if I had robbed her. But, it was not her fault; anyone could have mistaken me for a roadside *tapori*. Feeling a little unhappy, I turned back lest the people standing around think I was eve teasing her or something. Just then I heard her sweet voice, calling "Hey... Thank you." When I turned back, I saw that the words were meant for me, as she looked smilingly at me. I just stood there, looked at her, dumbfounded. I couldn't believe my ears. She had spoken to me. Yes...my dream girl had spoken to me.

I was thinking of something meaningful to say, but nothing came out. Finally I managed to croak, *"Ji.. ..k..koi baat nahi..."* But by that time the signal had turned green and she was off on her scooty in a second. Tongue-tied, I watched her zip down the road.

Evening: 7 pm

"Ya Allah At least today I should have got some money." But I was thankful to God for the blissful evening, as she had spoken to me for the first time today. Thank you *Allah*. It was the only beautiful moment that day, other than the pastry of course.

Ewww ewww eww....Three people were standing on the opposite side of the road. They were dressed in white shirts and trousers, wearing thick golden chains round their necks, bracelets, golden rings in their fingers; they looked menacing, like characters straight out of some gangster movie. One of them had thrown a stone on Chhamiyaan. One of them threw a stone again. God knows what fun they were deriving out of this. The bloody *chutiyas*. Again threw a stone and started laughing. Chhamiyaan barked at them, but they kept throwing stones.

"Stop it *saab*. He is my dog." I said.

One of them, who was wearing gold framed sunglasses, came near me and said, "*Achha*, this is your dog... *to tu kya hai be... tu bhi to kutta hi hai.*"

I kept quiet. The *chashmish* walked further ahead. Chamiyaan was standing right besides me, barking at him. He stood in front of us and all of a sudden kicked Chhamiyaan. The poor dog let out a cry and limped away.

I said angrily, "*Saab*, now it's too much."

He said, "What will you do? What can you do? Go and fuck your dog."

"*Saab*, at least leave the animal." I said.

He got annoyed, "You rascal, I will beat the hell out of you now. How dare you argue with me?"

All three of them had gathered around me by now, and without any intimation, the *chashmish* started hitting me, the others also joined in. Both my dog and I were getting beaten up. We were totally helpless against them. *Allah*, never make anybody so weak. No one came to save us. Everyone there feared our assailants. I was lying on the ground, writhing in pain, but they showed no mercy. Then all of a sudden, four men appeared out of nowhere. They stopped the *chashmish* and the other two men. One of them apologised to *chashmish* on my behalf, and asked him to forgive me. With a lot of effort, those four people succeeded in saving me. I was breathing heavily by now and my eyes were full of tears. I managed to sit up, lowered my eyes, avoiding contact with the crowd there.

One of the four people, who had saved me, came near and said, "My name is Dinesh. Consider me your friend. Meet me behind Richardson Mill at 11.30 in the night."

Saying this, he left.

I was engrossed thinking about the whole episode till 11 pm. I didn't have the desire to eat. The bruises had swollen up and were paining a lot. But the question that was bothering me was that he had called me at 11.30. Should I go? Then I remembered that they had saved me when I was in trouble, I should at least meet them.

So, I headed towards Richardson Mill.

Richardson is an old Mill. Situated next to J.J.Hospital, it's been closed for many years. It occupies a large amount of land in this already crowded area of Byculla. It was a very secluded place and hardly anyone entered those premises.

As I walked towards the Mill, I could almost feel everyone looking at me. Bystanders talked to each other in hushed tones as I passed by. I was feeling even more ashamed. Everyone was watching me as if they knew me, their sympathizing looks made me recollect the beating that I had taken, as if I was some animal. I hadn't been able to hit back and that made me even more dejected. I was so engrossed in the thought that I didn't realize I had reached the place behind Richardson Mill.

It was a small *gully* behind the Mill compound. Those four people were already standing there. There was a deathly silence, nobody spoke. I stepped towards them slowly. Dinesh signalled me to hide behind a wall with the other three. I obeyed him. Dinesh stood there in the open, alone. I was clueless about the whole episode. Then I saw that the same *chashmish*, who had beaten me in the afternoon, come walking through the lane in a drunken gait. He was alone. Watching him, I feared being trapped by these four people and the *chashmish*. I had no idea what was to come next. So, I kept an eye on the three guys standing next to me. I stood in a casual manner, but ready to run away from there.

Suddenly, Dinesh called me, "Javed, is he the same rascal who had beaten you up?"

Surprised, I came out of the hiding place and replied, "Yes."

Chashmish had reached the place and tried to run away on seeing Dinesh, but he was hardly able to walk as he was very drunk and Dinesh caught hold of him by his shirt collar. I got scared too.

Dinesh said, "Javed, you move little away. I want to talk to him personally."

I turned back and started walking to where the others were standing.

I was alert, as I still didn't trust them. I was just a few feet away from the rest of three, when I heard a muffled scream. All the three, standing in front of me were looking towards Dinesh, unblinkingly. When I turned back, I saw that Dinesh had stabbed the *chashmish* in his abdomen with a chopper and was holding his mouth tightly shut. He pulled the chopper further down, ripping his stomach. Both of them were drenched in red. I wanted to stop Dinesh, but the other three stopped me from doing so.

Finally, that *chashmish* died. After watching all this, I felt giddy and fell to the ground.

The night was silent. I had barely regained my senses when I heard the hooter blare. The sound was coming from the nearby Mazgaon dock, signalling midnight.

That day had turned out to be my real birthday. A new Javed was born.

3

SHAK....WHAT THE F_CK.

Next morning

It was another hot day as usual, as I stood there at my usual place with my key stack in hand. Eyes were heavy, deprived of sleep in the night gone by. It wasn't as if I had been awake without a wink of sleep. I did feel sleepy. But the moment my eyes closed, the shining blade of Dinesh's dagger would flash in front of my eyes and my eyes would open wide awake. I could see the murder taking place before my eyes, again and again. It was almost theatrical. Dinesh was right there, standing in front of me in his immaculate white shirt and jeans, with the dagger in hand and a cold hatred in his eyes. Blood splattered across his shirt and face, as the shining blade pierced my chest.

It was at this moment that I woke up, with a jolt. Me! Why did it have to be me? Why was I seeing this? Everything was the same, except that I was getting murdered. I shuddered at the very thought. But, why would Dinesh want to kill a penniless, harmless loner like me. Surely my mind was playing tricks on me. The truth was that I was shocked by the events of last evening. I had witnessed a murder right in front of my eyes a few hours back. Somehow, I feared violence. The streets of Mumbai were yet to convince me to accept violence as part and parcel of daily life.

The sun was high in the afternoon sky. I sat in my corner, red-eyed, still waiting for my first customer. Just then, I noticed a familiar face walking towards me along the street. I strained my eyes and could make out that the person was Dinesh. He called out to me. He was dressed very oddly though. An old, faded white shirt with upturned sleeves, grey trousers and slippers. Something was pulling the collar of his shirt backwards; it was an umbrella resting on the back of his collar, I later realized. It swayed merrily as its owner ambled casually on the footpath as if without a care in the world. I was lost for words as he greeted me, "Hey Javed *bhai*, what's up?"

"What the fuck man! How can you just roam about like this after what happened last night? I thought you might be underground by now. Go and hide somewhere. The *mama log* must be after you." I said.

"What happened last night, Javed? Nothing. Everything has been covered up. The *mama log* won't even get a sniff about what happened, they don't stand a chance! You shouldn't be worrying about these things when we are around."

"But don't you think what happened last night was wrong?" I asked.

- "Who gives a damn about right or wrong here man! Mumbai doesn't care about right or wrong Javed. It's just about who is and who isn't. Look at yourself, you think what I did is wrong, but you have followed the 'right' path throughout your life, then how come you landed up here, on this footpath, with no place to live, no friends, except for a filthy dog, scrambling for food..both of you..."

"Don't call him filthy, he is my Chhamiyaan...." I retorted.
- "Ok whatever, you and your Chhamiyaan. Someday, some rich brat's car will crush you to death at this very signal. That would be the end of your story, Javed. Nobody cares if you live or die."

I had known very few good people in my life, and hardly had anyone ever shown concern about my well being. And here was this guy, who had committed a murder the night before, but was concerned about me. Harsh though his words were, he had spoken the truth. What was I? A nobody. No one would care even if I were to die tomorrow. Then why should I care about what is wrong and what is right.

Soon we were joined by the other three persons from last night's meeting…Dinesh's friends. They greeted Dinesh warmly and hugged him; they met him like long lost friends. There was plenty of laughter, pats, *de taalis* and some good natured leg pulling, the main subject of which was the biggest guy of the lot, who talked in some incomprehensible language which only the other three understood, and enjoyed, as was evident from their laughter.

Meanwhile, Dinesh turned their attention towards me. "Friends," he said. "This is Javed, master key maker. He will be our companion from now on." then he proceeded to introduce the other three to me "This is Toya, Santosh and Aadesh. We…."

"Whaof, whaw, whaw!!" Suddenly there was a lot of commotion as Chhamiyaan appeared from nowhere and started barking fiercely at the four men. I immediately bent down and tapped him on his head and sent him away.

"I'm sorry guys; I don't know what came over Chhamiyaan so suddenly, he is normally very calm and composed."

"He'll do well as a police dog!" chuckled Santosh as we shook hands.

"Hi Taved, wel tome to the tloop." said the big guy.

"Don't mind him, his tongue slips over everything, he says… welcome to the group." said Aadesh, smiling.

"No, no, really, I …… er.. understood."

They all laughed. I joined in too. For the first time in my life, I was with friends. I was a part of some group. Brothers in arms.

One doesn't realise how quickly time passes when with friends. I was with them till the evening, during which I also did the work of making duplicate keys for 6 locks and also opened a suitcase. All credit to my friends who brought the clients to me.

They were quite like me. Trying to emerge from poverty, but they were more determined than me to make a life for themselves. I was barely managing to make ends meet, the quest for a life full of riches and luxury was way beyond me and I had almost given up, but somewhere in my heart, there was still a desire to be happy and rich. People said money can't buy riches, but there were so many other things that money could buy, they never said anything about that. Meeting these people had rekindled that desire in my heart. That is why I shared a good rapport with them. But surely they were unique, everyone..one of a kind.

Starting with Toya, the mystery man cum giant. The way he talked seemed rather mysterious. To a new listener it might seem that he was talking in some foreign language, even I was stumped for a moment when I first heard him speak. Later he explained that he had a lisp. Otherwise, he was a scary specimen, well over six feet tall, broadly built, his face bore scars from his previous fights. He could easily manhandle two to three people at a time and formed a major part of the gang's defence system. And the rest were real scoundrels to make fun of him every time he spoke a word. I didn't like that, but I felt Toya didn't mind, he knew his friends well. I respected their friendly affection and the ability of others to decode Toya's language too. Another mystery associated with Toya was his name. I mean there are many uncommon names but why did his parents choose an unearthly name like 'Toya' was a mystery to me. But later I got to know that his real name was 'Bhimsen' surely typifying him. 'Toya' was the name that was given to him because of his craving for soda. I had heard that 'desire' of the other kind is often the reason behind a person's name being spoilt, but in his case the name was spoiled literally. He loved drinking soda very much and because of lisp, he called it 'Toya'. I was exasperated on hearing that. The local shopkeeper used to get frustrated showing him a hundred ways of calling it 'soda'. But then as time moved on, Toya became a regular customer to him and the result was that now even the shop owner called 'Soda' as 'Toya', when Toya asks for it. Watching this 'Toya'ful conversation between them, the passers by used to think the gigantic man's name to be 'Toya' and that's how this myth started.

Next in the group was Santosh, our local. He was the simplest of the lot, both in dressing style and nature, and was a likeable fellow. He was a native of Mau village in Uttar Pradesh. He had a good physique, the result of working out for hours at the Colaba gym. And I got to know that he knew karate too, the art that helped him to survive several street fights. Dinesh and Santosh were best friends, or to still better, they were like brothers to each other. They first met each other in the local gym, supporting each other to lift heavy weights, eventually the friendship grew stronger, and now they were inseparable.

Dinesh was a simple guy and stayed in Colaba chawl. He too had tough muscles with the cuts in the required locations, unlike mine. He was about to get into police force, but some officer asked him for a bribe of fifty thousand rupees, which he couldn't manage and was thus rejected in medical examination. Though he seemed to be a quiet guy, he actually opened up as we got to know each other better. He was a short-tempered guy, who didn't fear anyone.

Last, but surely not the least was Aadesh. One word would describe him perfectly- hero. A fair guy with a great athletic body and good height; he looked like a foreigner. A real charmer, well versed in English, trained to influence girls and always dressed in stylish modern clothes. He was the youngest and the most knowledgeable member of the group. That's why he was given the job to plan for every con. In short, he was the brain behind the gang's activities. Aadesh stayed with his mom in a small place near Kalbadevi, his dad had died a few years back. Dinesh told me how Aadesh had joined the gang. The story was quite interesting too. He used to rob the affluent people residing around the Navy Nagar area. Even the navy men often fell prey to his perfect con jobs, and the police were left clueless. That area came under the territory of the other three. They got to know about it and tried to nab him in various ways but he escaped every time. Eventually, they managed to nab him, thanks to their *punter log*. Even after being caught, Aadesh didn't fear and instead he told them to take him into the gang, assuring them that they could work wonders together; his brains and the strength and contacts of the others. Santosh and Dinesh weren't able to overlook his confidence and since that day, he had been working with the gang.

Santosh, Dinesh and Aadesh studied in Sidhharth College of Arts. Toya had never in his life gone to any school or college. His life was dedicated to exercising in his *Akhada*.

These four did the job of recovering people's money, sometimes officially for banks and sometimes unofficially for the *baniyas*. They were also into illegal crimes like robbing. Their best loot till date was the Godrej loot, when they had looted a salary van of that company. They had been in jail too, quite a few times, but thanks to Dinesh's police training I-card, they were released without much inquiry. And, as I had seen, they had committed at least one murder. I didn't bother asking how many more people they had killed.

I was enjoying life in their company. We often roamed around in malls, restaurants and cinema halls, but spent most of the time at our regular *chai tapri*. Whenever we visited any theatre, they never stood in queue for ticket. They used to put their hand in at the ticket window directly. Looking at Toya, no one would raise voice against them.

The ticket seller though would be in a fix, try to interpret Toya's version of the name of the movie. Watching me with them, people now respected me too. But I never misused that advantage, nor did I ever support them in any of their 'jobs'. I was still living my own simple, straightforward life. But that was to change, soon.

One fine evening 4 pm

All of us were sitting at a nearby *chai tapri*, having our customary evening *chai* and chatting merrily. It was always fun to have these guys around.

Santosh raised his glass of *chai* towards me and said, "Hey Javed, so when are you planning to join us man. You will earn a lot with us, you know that."

"No *bhai*, I think I am fine as I am. I would rather be your friend than partner." I said.

Aadesh cut me off, "Oh yes bro..what an idea! Javed, you make keys, right? Well, that's all you will have to do dude, make duplicates, but for us."

"Whatever! What if I get caught?" I retorted.

- "How are you gonna get caught? You will be nowhere in the picture dude. We are the ones who are gonna make the loot. You only have to provide us a duplicate of the duplicate that you have made."

Aadesh talked with the confidence that gave me the feeling that he had already made up his mind.

- "And you know what, it's not as if we are gonna rob the poor of their life's savings. A few lakhs is nothing for these rich buggers. It's like taking a bucketful of water from the ocean, and no one will be harmed."

Dinesh and Santosh nodded in agreement.

Toya spluttered, "Whath Taved, you wonth thu thith muth fol uth *kya*?"

They were all coaxing me to get into their gang and I was somehow fighting the urge to agree with them.

"Enough guys, it's about time for my evening prayers, I gotta go."

I took their leave hurriedly and walked briskly towards the J.J signal.

She was there, waiting for the signal to go green, as I reached. Actually, the *namaaz* was just an excuse. I couldn't bear to miss seeing her. In this hard, unforgiving world, the mere sight of her, even if for only a few moments, would come as a whiff of fresh air. Her long brown hair flying in the wind, her beautiful bright skin glowing in the sunshine and her brown eyes matching perfectly with her hair. I would be stoned even if she threw a cursory glance at me, she was so beautiful. For more than three years now, this had become almost a ritual for me; watching her at the signal. I was distraught when *chacha* had died four years back and was on the verge of committing suicide myself, when I first saw her at the same place. In more than one way, she was the reason I was alive, she was my solace.

I was lost watching her, when Aadesh came and sat beside me.

Aadesh "What bro, so this is your *namaaz*."

I didn't hear him, but my gaze gave him a clue regarding whom I was watching.

He continued, "Item *sahi hai* bro. What curves *yaar*. I'll make her mine someday."

"Shut up you idiot, she is mine. She will be your sister-in-law." I snapped at him.

Aadesh "Oh sorry bro, I had no idea about that. I thought you were just feasting your eyes."

I looked at him with raised eyebrows.

"By the way, have you ever spoken to her in this regard, or just having a thought?"

- "No, not yet. I don't even know her name. Just know that I love her."

Aadesh, "He he, Why would she tell you her name? You are just a poor key maker and in this world nothing matters but money. That's why buddy, work with us. And then see, you will have money, style and status. A girl doesn't expect anything more than that. Just imagine, you and this girl are on a bike at this very signal, she is holding you tightly and talking to you with a smile. *Bass*, watching you there every one will die out of jealousy. Then you laugh at them with pride. Trust me dude, your dream will become the reality of your life."

Those words raised a spark of hope in me "Aadesh, you are right." but I still doubted its practicality "It's not so easy. Getting away after a theft comitted with the help of a duplicate key is not so easy. The police know about the number of key makers in the area, because they are the ones who allot us the license. Here's mine."

Aadesh observed my license for a minute, reading every single letter over it and said, "Ok, anything more?"

The plan wasn't practically possible, but I wanted to explain the whole scenario to Aadesh, as I believed in his intelligence "And yes, we have to maintain a record book for the work done. In that, we have to write the addresses where we made the key, the person's name and have to take their signature. Whenever there is a theft in the locality, police ask us first."

Listening to all that, Aadesh closed his eyes for sometime, probably to think. Then he said, "Javed, do you consider me your friend."

Now, that was an absurd question at this point of time, while I was expecting some solution to the problem "Yes, indeed."

"Then don't worry, I have a foolproof plan. The thefts will be comitted with a duplicate key and you will be safe too, for sure."

I was silent, showing compliance and ignored the query of the exact plan.

But then I realised, "*Abey*, how will I make the duplicates. I mean...the person who wants the key to be made will be standing next to me. If I make an extra duplicate in front of him, wouldn't he ask me?"

Aadesh, "Everything's arranged bro. Take this."

He handed me a small rectangular box, which was filled with some doughy material. I asked him what it was.

Aadesh, "This is clay, the same clay that children use for playing to make animals, houses, tables, etc and now this clay will help us mould our future. You just have to take an impression of the key on it, and it can be done within a flash. Isn't it great?"

To check its efficacy, I made impressions of several keys and saw that it made an absolutely perfect imprint. And surely it would make the work easier.

For the next few weeks, I was quite busy with my new job. I kept on making duplicate keys for rich people and my friends kept on emptying their lockers. These people used to make me stand with my key stall at far off places like Ghatkopar, Mulund, Ulhasnagar and Andheri, not in my Umer khadi. And that too near plush societies and far from the police station, so that the police would rarely come there. The duration between the key work and robbery was at least one month to avoid suspicion. Aadesh made the duplicate licenses for me; it was simple as it was just an ordinary printout. By the way, hats off to their information network. Every second or third day, someone or the other would come to get a key made, wherever these people placed me.

The only thing to worry about was the police, but they had a solution for that too. If any police officer asked me, I would show him the fake license and on that day itself, I would vacate the spot. Also, the moment they set off on any robbery, I would leave that area. The change in location was accompanied by a change in disguise too.

The result of my work was showing its effect. With stylish clothes, glares and an attitude, I used to sit at my stall. I have been using a lot of perfume these days, that too the foreign ones. But yes, I didn't show off too much as it would be an invitation to unnecessary suspicion. Chhamiyaan has got style too; roams about wearing a collar, chasing female dogs. By the way, even I saw my girl after some days, but this time I saw her in my new avatar very different from my earlier ragged one. Really, its fun to have money. Life was set, but then one day *Allah* did something to me that made my eyes wet.

Morning 10 am

"Hey boy, can you make a duplicate key for a cupboard locker?" a thin man dressed in a watchman's uniform asked, eyeing me suspiciously.

I had just had a heavy breakfast. "Yes sure." I said, but didn't show much interest as I wasn't in the mood to go about tinkering some old watchman's locker.

"Then come to *saab's* place. You are required there, urgently."

"Where is it?" I asked.

He said, "Room no. 213, sixth floor, Samson Apartments, and yes…come quickly."

I picked up my tools and set off; it was going to be an interesting job.

Samson Apartments was the abode of the rich. It was the tallest building in Umer khadi. They say you can see upto Grant road station from its terrace. But the most notable feature for me was the many rich and beautiful girls who lived here.

I was visiting that apartment for the first time and as if by some divine intervention, a tall, young, skimpily clad girl emerged out of the foyer of the apartment as I entered the gate. She was wearing ultra short and tight shorts, so small, in fact, that the underwear I was wearing was longer. Her long, fair legs gleamed as they were exposed to the sun. She wore a *ganji* like thing on top, which was again small and tight fitting; I could see her belly button quite clearly. However, big round glasses that resembled those that people wore after an eye operation almost covered her face. In no time, she walked towards a car, got into it and was off in a tick.

These rich people are always in a hurry, only *fukat* people like us have all the time in the world. Her beauty was lost on me though; she was nothing compared to my girl. Short clothes were nothing but a waste of money for me, the real beauty of a girl lies in her eyes, and the rich lass had covered her eyes. Not my type, as Aadesh would have said.

The watchman guided me to the lift. It was like some mini *sheesh mahal*. Glass on all four sides, bright lighting, a hidden fan somewhere in the ceiling, music in the background, and a sweet girl's voice guiding me through the floors. I was busy setting my hair, looking into the mirror, as I always did that looking at my reflection, when the sweet voice said, "Sixth floor." This was where I had to get out. I got out hurriedly after the door opened and barely survived slipping over the smooth floor. The flooring of the corridor was ultra smooth and my old plastic sandals hardly found any grip over it. The result was that, I almost slipped over the floor and almost fell. An aunty walking past me regarded me with disdain and got into the lift. She must have recognized me as an outsider.

Finally, I reached there. 213, written over a big door, in gold. The nameplate said 'Dr.Dipen Sinha'. I looked for the clevis to knock, but found none. I smiled to myself, realising it wasn't some Umer khadi chawl room and rang the door bell at the right, then rang it again, I liked the sound of it.

A guy opened the door, I had seen him somewhere, his face looked familiar.

"Who are you?" he asked.

"Javed, *saab*, key maker; you sent the watchman to call me", I replied.

- "Ya ya. Come in."

He proceeded hurriedly towards a big Godrej cupboard in what looked like his bedroom. I followed him. He opened it and showed me the locker "I want a duplicate key for this locker and I want it quick, ok?"

I opened my tool bag, took out the bunch of raw keys, the filing tool and the wooden block and set to work. It was gonna be a tough job. Godrej lockers are always a headache, might even take upto 30-45 minutes. Meanwhile, I couldn't help but notice the picture of a semi-nude woman hanging on the adjoining wall. I tried not to stare at it but couldn't help stealing a few glances. Also, the room was nicely done, with an extra large television fitted on the wall, and it was cool too, may be the air conditioner was on. But, the room felt a bit warm after 10 minutes, may be because I was hard at work. Then I realised after a few minutes that he had turned off the air conditioner.

I had always dreamed of living in a house such as this. I was enjoying every moment of this tough job, the comfort of the expensive furniture, the marble floor on which I sat, had somehow set my pulse racing. I was working double fast. It is then I remembered that the boy was the same whom I had seen outside the bar that night, throwing bundles of cash on the bar manager. And yes, he was the same guy who was bribing that *hawaldaar* too.

It took me almost half an hour to complete the duplicate key for the locker. Phew! It was hard work. I had broken into mild sweat even in the lately airconditioned room. However, I sneaked a quick glance inside the locker without the boy noticing. Man! Was it a mini treasure chest? I could see boxes of jewellery sets and bundles of notes. I closed the door of the locker; acting as if I hadn't noticed a thing and gave the key to the guy.

"It's done *saab*, here's your key. *200 rupees ho gaya.*"

"*200 rupees? Itna kis baat ka?*"

These rich people really don't know where to save money and where to spend it. There at the bar counter, he was throwing cash as if it had no value and now he was haggling with me just for 200 rupees for my hard work. I was about to give him a piece of my mind, but controlled myself somehow and said, "Fixed rate sir, for coming to your place, making the duplicate."

Just then I heard a woman's voice through the doorway "C'mon Sashank. *De do na.* We need to go now, *jaldi karo*"

I looked at the direction from where the sweet voice came. She was there, standing at the door, she was my signal girl. I just sat there, staring at her open-mouthed. I could not make sense of her presence there. Surely she didn't stay in this house, or this apartment for that matter, or else I would have noticed that by now. What was she doing in this guy's place? And that too, just the two of them in the house. Could she be his girlfriend...? No no, they must be cousins or something. My head was spinning with questions. *Shak se apun ka dimag phat raha tha.*

4

SASHANK'S LIFE

"*2*00 *rupees? Itna kis baat ka?*"

The key-maker looked puzzled, as if charging 200 rupees for making a duplicate key was the most natural thing in the world. He had obviously taken one look at me and decided that I was rich. Little did he know that none of it belonged to me. My dad counted every rupee in his locker everyday, and this task of getting a duplicate key made for the locker was assigned to me only because he had some emergency to attend and obviously couldn't ask Mom to do it. They already had a fight over this. Otherwise, the locker was always out of bounds for me.

"C'mon Sashank, *de do na*. We need to go now. *Jaldi*." That was the voice of Priety..my…my …hmm…friend. I loved hearing my name on her lips.

So, let me introduce myself to you.

I am Sashank Sinha, the only son and punching bag of my dad, Dr.Sinha. Currently studying in the 4ᵗʰ and final year of EXTC engineering, for those who are not so technically inclined, EXTC is the short form of 'Electronics and telecommunications'.

Not so handsome, not so geeky; Simple living, high thinking is my way. Well, that's the only way that I can afford. My life is full of confusions. One such confusion that I cannot get my head over is the reason for my parents having me. I mean they don't love me. Hell, they don't even love each other! Other questions that have been troubling me for ages are

Why engineering?

Why not B.Sc with a B.Com girlfriend?

Why locker?

Why Priety?..

Oh yes..actually no...*pata nahin yaar*...I am still confused about the last question.

Life was static till a tornado named Priety came into my life - a tornado that swept me off my feet and took me along with it. She had brought a thrill and happiness into my life, not unlike a child who has no fears of falling on a swing.

It was five months back *Jab* we met. I had known her before that too. I mean, I'd seen her in college but never had the chance to speak to her in the last four years. But man, she was so beautiful! The fact was that I rarely interacted with most of my college mates. I restricted myself to my few near and dear friends most of the time. My dad is a doctor, but I had decided not to follow his footsteps and hence had taken up engineering, something, I wasn't too inclined to do earlier. Anyway, as our final year drew to a close, most of us became busy with our projects.

One cold day in January, as we sat huddled together in the college canteen, I and my friends, Rahul, Vicky and Shikha decided that it was high time we started working on our final project and got together to form a project group. But, we were still one person short. And, to my delight, Shikha suggested Priety's name.

We boys were like "Ok. Ask her if she's not anyone else's project…I mean, in anyone else's project group."

But, despite our outward nonchalance, we boys were excited and happy to let her join us. Man, she was the crush of at least a dozen boys in our college! But, the whole college knew that the girl was committed. I mean, she was in a serious relationship with someone for years. That someone was not from our college. That's why she was always seen stuck to her phone.

We had already started working on our project as we wanted to submit it early and also our final exams, which were scheduled in May, were fast approaching. Priety, who had gone to visit her hometown, joined us a few days later. Girls staying in hostel feel homesick now and then.

31st January

Vicky asked, "Hey guys, Priety was going to come today *na*…Where is she?"

Rahul answered, "Shikha and Priety will be coming late."

Vicky and Me, (surprised and angry) "How do you know?"

Rahul, "Don't worry guys, Shikha told me yesterday."

Vicky, "Hmm…Shikha told *haan*."

Rahul stared at Vicky, "*Haan*, Shikha told. And yes, Shikha is my girlfriend. Ok. Do you wanna argue about it now?"

After a brief silence, the three of us laughed sheepishly, actually at ourselves.

Shikha, "Hey, you people, concentrate on work."

Shikha had just arrived and Priety was with her. Boy, her looks were really something to die for.

Shikha "Let me introduce you guys to the newest member of our group. *Dhan te naan*. This is Priety Verma. I am sure you know her name already. She's just returned from her home in Pune."

One look at the young lady in cool blue jeans and a cute pink short *kurti* and all of us were over one another trying to introduce ourselves to her. Every boy was on his toes to explain the project to her. But, thanks to Shikha and my long standing image in my college, of being an innocent boy, the job was given to me. At that time, Vicky and Rahul's faces were worth a Kodak moment.

"Hi, I am Sashank. See, we are making a project on the topic 'MOBILE HOME CONTROL'. It's basically how a mobile phone can be used to control devices at home, when you are away. I mean to switch off lights, turn the a.c on, etc. Everything is controlled by Bluetooth or messaging...."

I don't know what rubbish I was telling her because unintentionally, I was just admiring her eyes, that *kajal,* her smile, the way she nodded and the sweet tinkling sound, her earrings made every time she nodded. It was as if, everything was in slow motion. While explaining to her the various uses of the mobile phone, I felt a little inferior as I was explaining it to a person who had been making the best use of it for years. I mean to speak to her boyfriend.

As days passed, we became good friends. One day, while I was writing the project report, my pen stopped working, although it was full of ink. I got frustrated and jerked it a couple of times but to no avail.

Words came naturally, "*Bhench*....What the fuck is this!"

A second later, I realised that Priety was sitting next to me.

"Sorry." I said, a little embarrassed.

Again, I started jerking the pen so that I could look busy. I was trying to avoid eye contact with her. I kept staring down at my desk till I could see the scratches on it clearly. As, I continued jerking the pen, my hand accidentally touched hers. Red faced, I apologised again.

She looked at me with an odd expression and said, "C'mon Sashank, 'fuck' is a usual word and I am not an untouchable to feel sorry. It's cool."

I gave a sigh of relief; she had not heard the first word. Her words boosted my confidence. I looked at her beautiful face, and we both smiled, giving me a clue of the progress in our friendship.

In about two weeks, we got accustomed to each other. We were always together. Changing the gear and speeding up our test ride, we reached the milestone of 'Good friends'. In our breaks, we sat isolated from the others and spoke in low voices.

Priety, "*Achha suno na*, can I ask you something?"

I guess I had an idea what she was going to ask. Girls always take permission before asking personal questions.

But I had nothing to hide. Confidently, I said, "Sure…go ahead."

- "Do you have a gf?"

Puzzled and ashamed at the same time, I said, "No"

She said, "It's ok. You will get someone someday." and smiled the way she used to smile every time our eyes met.

Some memories are such that I can't forget.

One such day was the day when she got angry at me for the first time. She was typing the project report and was tired working for the last 5 hours. I was late that day. Time was running out for us as we had to complete the project. So, I was charged to complete it as fast as we could. I was pumped up and wanted to boost everyone's confidence. So, I told them to work without any break. Listening to this, Priety got up and moved out of the room. I didn't notice that she was angry. Looking at the speed of her steps, I thought that she wanted to visit the rest room. This is where experience counts. After around 15 minutes she came back...totally changed. I swear, beautiful girls are great actors. She sat away from me indicating she was avoiding me. I was convinced of her anger when I tried to speak to her and she gave me monosyllabic answers.

I got the hint and asked, "What's the matter. What happened?"

Girls have a very bad habit of taking *maunvrath*. Taking some time, she explained the reason to me with a serious face and then it took me lot of apologies and an ice cream to calm her down. Finally, she was back with the drug I was addicted to....her smile.

That night, as I stared up at the star lit sky, all I could think about was her. In love, you are bound to do such stupid things. My phone rang "*Chhitti aayi hai aayi hai chhitti aayi hai*". That's my message tone. It was Priety's message. First message from her.

From: Priety

Hi..Priety here....Thank u for caring so much...You are my

special friend. Gn. Take care.

I just had to read it again.

Hi. Priety here. Thank you for caring so much. You are my special friend (Ohh..stepped one level ahead). Good night.

Take care (Those words and that too from her, made me feel my importance in her life). Yes. That small message was the first message from her. I was not used to such personal messages as I always got only non-veg messages from my friends.

I replied

Thank you. Good night. Take care. Sweet dreams. Keep smiling.

That came naturally. I tried to script every emotion I could in that short message.

I usually deleted such personal messages. But that day, I transferred that message from Priety into my 'Saved messages' folder. And then I slept.

I got up early the next day to get ready to meet her. Bathed thoroughly, wore ironed clothes, and sprayed myself generously using my favourite, Chocolate fragrance.

My phone rang. It was Priety's message

I have a severe headache.Going to clinic…Will come late…Will feel good if u can come.

My dad was a doctor. I knew the medicine for headache was

Diclofenac. But, I didn't want to miss the chance to spend time with her, alone. So, I replied

Ya sure… c u outside college campus in 5 mins…I am always there to take care☺

Kasam se that crappy last line was not at all intentional. It's the result of watching cheesy Indian movies. Having promised to meet her in 5 minutes, I got out of the apartment and took a cab.

Normally, it took 15 minutes to reach my college gate. But this driver was talented. I reached my college gate in 10 minutes. My eyes were searching for her. There she was, standing at the college gate, in a grey top and black jeans. She was looking weak. There were dark circles round her eyes, but still she looked beautiful. I don't know how she could manage to look awesome all the time.

I got out and helped her get in.

Me, "Don't worry Priety, we will reach Dr. Mehta's clinic in 10 minutes. His medicines work really fast."

Priety, "Hmm…ok".

With those words, she rested her head on my shoulders. I think it wasn't deliberate. I stayed still, no movements at all. The strands of her hair were bringing on a sneeze. But I controlled it. I didn't have the courage to meet her eyes. So, I started watching the sights outside the window. During the whole drive, the driver was looking at the rear view mirror.

I wanted the drive to continue forever. But, as all good things in this world have to come to an end, we reached the clinic in 15 minutes. The clinic wasn't very crowded. We entered the doctor's cabin. Throughout, I was holding Priety's hand. I helped her to the seat. Dr. Mehta had a typical doctorish personality with a bespectacled face. He had an amazing ability of interacting with the patients and making them feel confident and sure of getting cured. After diagnosing the symptoms, the doctor prescribed her Diclofenac, Rantac and multivitamins.

As soon as we came out of doctor's clinic, her phone rang *"Whatever you do, I'll be two steps behind you…wherever you go, and I'll be there to remind you…"* She left my hand, walked some distance away and answered the call. I could not hear the conversation. I didn't know whose call it was. She was speaking too softly for me to hear. It made me feel restless.

She was already feeling better on the way back. I didn't know whether it was because of the doctor or the call. Hence, unfortunately she didn't rest her head on my shoulders this time. But, she looked pensive. I rehearsed asking her the reason in my mind but couldn't find the courage to ask in actual words. Finally, I dropped her at the hostel and went to the college. All I could think the whole day was the call she had received in the clinic.

Night 10.30 pm

I was trying to concentrate on my studies. Going through the pages of 'Satellite communication or Satcom', I was lost in her thoughts. That call was still making me feel uneasy.

A thousand questions had sprung up in my mind in a second.

Whose call was it…Boyfriend's?

No no…might be from home.

I was lost in these, when Satellite communication came into action. I got a call from her.

Me, "Hello Priety. Are you ok now?"

Priety, "Yes Sashank. I am well now…..Have I disturbed you? Were you studying?"

Me "No no…not at all…what happened?"

Priety, *"Aise hi. Dinbhar se kuchh baat nahin huyi thi na."*

And then started the delight.

The initial hour of our conversation was on general topics..college, hostel, roommates and all. In the second hour we proceeded towards personal information questions.

Priety, "Hey, when is your birthday?"

Me, "5th June 1987. When's yours?"

Priety, "Hmm…u guess"

That was the most stupid question I'd ever been asked. How could I make a correct guess out of 365 options?

Me, "Ohhk…sorry *yaar*. I can't wait to hear it. I don't want to waste time making guesses."

Priety "What an intelligent escape… who taught you that? You seem experienced in talking to girls. Ok…it's 4th April 1985"

The moment she said that, the date entered my brain like a virus that couldn't be removed. I noted that she was 2 years older to me. May be that's why I always obeyed her…haha.

My phone was getting warmer by the minute, as it was not used to such lengthy calls, also I had started sweating around my ear, but Priety was unstoppable. I am sure, if someone would have tapped our call and heard carefully, he would have heard my voice, all that I spoke was…..*haan, nahin, thik hai, achha, aur kya*, ok, ha haha, yes.

Priety, "Oh.oh….wait a minute. Oh *yaar*."

I heard a noise as if something had fallen.

Me, "What happened. Are you alright?"

Priety, "Haha. I just fell off the stool. Everyone in the hostel is sleeping. So, I just switched off my room lights and forgot that I was sitting on the stool. Ohh. Achha Sashank. Tell me. Who was your first crush in our college?"

Me, "Seriously speaking, I am sort of introvert. I've hardly spoken to any girl. By the way, what about you? You have a boyfriend *na*?"

That needed a lot of courage.

Priety, "*Haan*..How do you know?"

Me, "Everyone in the college knows about it."

Priety, "Okkk..yes. I have a boyfriend. His name is Hari.. Hari Iyer. We were in the same school. He was my senior. He proposed to me when I was in 9th and he was in 10th std. It's been 7 years and we are in a serious relationship. He is doing his MBA in Bangalore. I love him a lot."

Those words tore me apart. I mean, tore my heart.

For the next few minutes, I couldn't follow what she was talking about. But then..

Priety, "Sashank..Sashank..are you there?"

Me, "Yaa.*haan.*"

Priety, "*Suno na*, tomorrow, a senior friend of mine is coming to meet me. She wants me to be with her all day. Can you meet me tomorrow morning at J.J Juice Centre at 10."

Me, "Ya sure."

Before we knew it, it was 5.30 am.

Finally, as the sun rose, we wished each other good night and went to sleep.

Next day 10.30 am

As always, she was late. I was waiting for her at J.J Juice Centre. It is the most famous juice centre in Byculla, next to J.J Hospital. They have a unique collection of juices, which tasted like nector in the hot climate of March. It was crowded most of the time, partly because there was no other better juice centre around and partly because it was a very small shop, even three people present made it crowded.

Priety and her friend came. Her friend was really good looking. But, Priety has always seemed incomparable to me. Both of them ordered watermelon juice. I ordered a pineapple juice. We made some small talk till the time the juice arrived. By the time the juice was served, Priety had described to me the history of their friendship. I was least interested to know about it. But, I made every attempt to conceal that. After straining my neck muscles to nod a few times, I felt relieved as the waiter approached us with the 3 big goblets filled with juice. I handed the watermelon juice glasses to the ladies and picked up mine. It's called manners. And *haan*, in this modern world, where no one differentiates between a man and a woman, it is an accepted fact that only a man is expected to display his manners.

She told me to taste the watermelon juice which she had ordered. I extended my hand to a bunch of straws. She stopped me silently and told me with her loving eyes, to share the same straw. I hated watermelon juice, but somehow I liked it when she offered it to me. There I felt the warmth of love once again. It made me feel special. Priety's friend noticed this whole drama, but she feigned ignorance. Now, I think that is manners too.

With time, our relationship strengthened. We cared for each other.

We watched movies, spent hours at McDonalds and CCD. During this period, I lied the most to my friends. My phone bill was full of calls to her. Vodafone was hurting in that aspect.

3rd April 11.50 pm

Her birthday was on the next day. I wanted to be the first one to wish her. I called her at 11.58 p.m. but, I only heard this.. "*The airtel number you are calling is busy on another call. Please try after sometime or stay online.*"

So I messaged her..

Happy birthday to you. many many happy returns of the day. may God shower loads of happiness on you. u seem busy. So messaged u. keep smiling. tc gn.☺

She replied.

Thank u.. ☺

That's how the moment went, a moment I had waited for months. Sometimes you feel like laughing at yourself. I felt the same, that night.

I experienced a different aspect of love a few days later. We had enrolled for a salsa workshop. Don't be surprised, I agreed only because Priety insisted and assured me that I wouldn't make a fool of myself. The trainer asked me to hold her hand and put the other hand on her waist. I was really nervous and kept my hand some centimeters away from her waist.

She said, "Sashank, you don't require my permission to put your hand on my waist. I was the one who convinced you into doing this, I trust you. You are my closest friend."

There I moved another step ahead, not in the dance but in our relationship, from being her special friend to closest friend. But, the word "FRIEND" was still there.

We enjoyed the dance. I don't know who discovered the salsa, but I surely appreciate his talent to innovate a dance for which the basic requirement is to be a couple. And, if you would have noticed, I have assumed the discoverer to be a male by default, as only men can rack their brains to find means to get near a woman.

But, one thing was pricking me the whole evening. Other people were staring at her because she wore a low necked T-shirt. So, to be frank, her cleavage was visible. My eyes were busy exploring her inner beauty. I mean the beauty of her soul that I always experienced whenever she came close to me. Still, if you don't believe me, I was busy looking at her face, into her eyes. But still I was feeling a bit uncomfortable. I was in a fix about telling her about it. But, as I cared for her, while returning, I mentioned it to her and told her that I wasn't comfortable with this.

She heard me out patiently. And then, she took me to one side, holding my arm gently and replied, "Sashank. I like you. I will take care of it the next time."

I kept my hands gently on her shoulders and said, "Thank you. I like you too. Be always as you are."

Days passed by, as we were busy with our project. Vicky, Rahul and Shikha were also frustrated with the project work. I too was frustrated. But not so much, as I had Priety's company all the time. We surfed the internet most of the time, getting information for our project. We were all desperate to complete the project. Also the date for the final exams .....16th May was fast approaching.

5

5TH MAY - 16TH MAY
JAVED'S VERSION

5th May, 11.15 am

Could she be his girlfriend…No no, they must be cousins or something. Jealousy flooded my thoughts like rains in Mumbai. *Shak se apun ka dimag phat raha tha.*

I turned around to get a glimpse of her just as the door was shut with a bang. I stood there for a few seconds like a confused child. I held the money tightly and felt dizzy as the world started to spin around me. I leaned on the wall for support and climbed down the stairs. My head was full of questions and everything else seemed very insignificant. I never realised when the six floors went by. I was oblivious to the lobby which seemed so luxurious moments ago. I went to my footpath corner and sat down. Chhamiyaan sat beside me, perhaps knowing how sad I was.

That's when I saw Dinesh and the rest of the gang coming from the other side.

"Hey Javed *bhai*, got any new job for us?" Santosh asked.

- "Huh...sorry.. didn't get you..."

"Haha, I meant have you got any new keys around for us to raid?"

I could hear him but all my thoughts were stuck at that girl and the stranger with her.

"I got no new work," I lied.

"*Theek hai yaar*.." Dinesh quipped. "We already have a work planned for 16th May; at Ghatkopar.....hey I just remembered.. Aadesh, you are coming along, right?"

"No, I can't make it. I need to take care of my mother. She's ill." Aadesh said in a low voice, with a sad face.

"Oh.. what happened?" I exclaimed.

"*To kab batayega saale.. Chal* .. It's alright; you stay back and take care of your mother." Dinesh said.

They made some plans for the next day and left.

I couldn't concentrate on my work for the coming week. Even the radio played sad songs all the time. Her thoughts occupied my mind constantly. I used to avoid the traffic signal for fear of seeing her. At times, I thought of confronting her, but later on realised it's not her fault – She was so beautiful, anyone could fall for her. I felt like killing that guy.

16th May 9.23 am

I woke up early. Lately I had not been sleeping well, it was almost time for me to open shop but instead I left for the *chai tapri* to meet my friends. They had already finished their tea and were just about to leave when I reached.

Santosh said, "Javed, we are leaving. We need to finish the Ghatkopar deal. Dinesh, Toya..let's go."

Toya, "I am leady tint llong. You only make uth late. *Yaal,* let's trink Toya tefore we leave."

Santosh and Dinesh laughed at that.

Dinesh, "*Abey* Toya, its 'soda', not 'toya'…haha. Bye Javed, wish us luck."

I bade them goodbye, in return.

Nowadays, I had become plain lazy. But shrugging off my laziness, I took a bath at the *khadi* tap today. It's been long since I had one. I fed Chhamiyaan and somehow managed to make one, actually two keys in the afternoon. Normally I wouldn't have broken a sweat for such an easy job, but it is difficult to work when your mind is preoccupied.

11.45 am

I was at the signal trying to forget her. There was the usual rush and traffic at the signal, sitting there I wondered how many different thoughts might be going on in the minds of all these people waiting here, some busy with their work, some in a hurry to reach their destination, some in cars, others on bikes, all different from each other, yet similar. All were simply waiting, ironically for the same thing – for the green signal. Except for the kids, they were out here earning their meal at the signal – selling newspapers, toys, etc. Like them, even I used to wait for it to turn red. Shit! No matter how much I tried to forget, I didn't succeed.

Aadesh arrived.

"What's wrong?" he inquired.

"Nothing." I lied.

He knew something was wrong. "Javed, you consider me your friend, right. C'mon tell me."

I didn't intend to tell him the facts, but then the guy came at the signal in his car; the same guy who was with her in the flat.

"Do you see that guy in the car?" I asked Aadesh.

'Hmmm … the one in the i20," he replied.

"The guy in the second row! Can't you see him?" I retorted.

Aadesh, still confirming "Ya, ya.. the same guy, blue t-shirt, in the white car, right?"

I nodded.

"What about him?" he asked. "Who is he?"

I told Aadesh about how I had seen her at this guy's flat, and that the way she had talked implied that they were quite close.

"When did this happen? Why were you there, in the first place?" Aadesh asked.

"I'd been there to make keys for his locker. That guy is very rich. Name's Sashank." I muttered.

Aadesh laughed, "He's got the girl coz he has the money, buddy. Money talks."

We sat there silently; I trying to cope with agony and Aadesh trying to think of a way for my happiness. After thinking for a while, he finally suggested we rob his place. "Once the money is gone, the girl will be free. Then, you can impress her and you will have the money." Aadesh advised.

But, I still could see a hurdle *"Nahi yaar Aadesh!* After the theft is committed, the police will come to me first, for inquiry. This area has only a couple of key-makers, and I am one of them. The police will surely inquire, then what…I will be caught."

Aadesh, "Buddy, when are you going to use the image that you have after being honest for so many years. This is the perfect time to use it. Listen, the police here know you for your honesty, do you agree with this?"

How could a person appreciate his own quality? Gently, I said "Yes."

Aadesh, "Then don't worry, just keep up the confidence to lie."

"Lie?" I hesitated.

- "At least that much you have to do, if you want that girl to be in your life....loving you, just imagine."

I could see his plan working. I had always dreamt of getting her attention and make a great impression.

"Do you think this would really work? What if she loves him? She would be hurt. I don't feel this is right. I wouldn't want to hurt her." I said.

"You are nuts. She'd be glad to have you. I know girls. Trust me on this. We have a perfect plan." Aadesh replied.

I still wasn't convinced.

-"Javed, life never gives you opportunities by itself. It is a race. If you slow down, the others will run over you. You will not get another opportunity like this. To win, you will have to push him down to run over him, in one way or the other." Aadesh explained.

His words and the confidence in his voice had spurred me; I could imagine my dream being accomplished, as half the work was already done. I was ready with the duplicate key to Sashank's locker. The con was on.

6

5TH MAY - 16TH MAY
SASHANK'S VERSION

5th May 11.30 am

"C'mon Sashank, *de do na*. We need to go now. *Jaldi*." That was the voice of Priety..my...my ...hmm...friend. I loved hearing my name on her lips.

I paid the key maker without any bargaining. He walked rather slowly and looked puzzled. I closed the door with a bang as soon as he left. We didn't have much time. The project was finally complete. Shikha, Rahul and Vicky were to meet us at college by 12 noon.

Priety, "You kept everything in your bag, right....the project report and the notes. Show me once."

Girls do have a few good habits. They make sure that you don't forget anything.

Priety, "Listen, you remember our plan *na*?"

We had planned to visit Worli sea face after submission to spend some time together, only the two of us. "Yes, ofcourse."

We moved out of the house and got into the lift. Waiting to descend six floors, I leaned on a wall of the lift; Priety reprimanded me for that. I stood straight right away. Priety was standing besides me and going through some papers while I was busy gawking at her reflection in the adjacent mirror. She was wearing a wide necked navy blue *kurti* with beautiful white embroidery, and white leggings. Her *kurti* was almost skin fit, as were the leggings, and they accentuated her perfect figure. I couldn't help staring at her and just hoped that she wouldn't notice. She was wearing pointed heels; I wondered what could be the reason to wear them at a project submission! Maybe she just liked to dress up.

"Ground floor" the sweet female voice announced. I stopped staring and moved out before her. We came out of the building compound and took a taxi that had just dropped Mr.Kapoor, my neighbour. After scrutinizing my companion with wide eyes, Mr.Kapoor looked at me and gave a wicked smile. I was sure he might have thought that Priety I and were going around. I just hoped he would keep his mouth shut like a good neighbour. But that wasn't to be.

By the time we reached college, it was 12.20. Rahul, Vicky and Shikha were already there. After checking the project for the last time, we went to our professor and submitted it.

We had prepared most of the points together and had almost equal knowledge about the project. We hoped that the vivas would turn out to be good. As we had decided earlier, the people going in for the viva first would later message the questions to the rest, sitting outside, as they weren't allowed to talk to us after the viva. Everything was going fine, quite a few questions were repeated by the examiner, it seemed. I was the last person to go in and hoped to reap maximum benefit from my batchmates' experience. But alas, that was not to be. Shikha was the one who had gone for the viva before me and as with everybody else; she had totally frustrated the examiner, who then decided to vent his ire on me. My viva lasted for almost 25 minutes; the examiner went into the depths of the project while I struggled to keep afloat. He questioned me about the practical application of the technology of our project in our country where electricity was almost a luxury, with all the load shedding and stuff. I answered him to my satisfaction about the practical applications; however, it was the very basics of the topic in which he took me to task. Finally, he gave me a frustrated look and said, "Go." I was waiting to hear those words for a long time; I thanked him and went out. The project had been finally submitted.

We met outside the college and discussed the questions; it turned out that many of us had given different answers to the same question, no wonder the examiner was frustrated. Priety's was the best viva, it seemed. We had a good laugh over our absurd answers. But, all of us were feeling the same emotion…happiness with a sigh of relief.

Engineering is like a hurdle race. When you cross one, another is ready to challenge you.

"Shit man.. The final exams are on 16th May. Only 11 days are left..*bamboo lagne wali hai,*" Rahul said as we moved out of the college and further went on to explain his words with the appropriate hand gesture. I indicated him to stop it; the girls watched and gave wry smiles.

We all were about to leave. Everything was going according to the plan. But, it was Vicky who came up with an idea that compelled me to lie.

Vicky said, "C'mon guys. Let's go for a movie. We have finally submitted our project!! It's time for celebration. Let's have fun today. We can study after that."

Priety and I sent a worried look at each other.

I interrupted quickly, "No *yaar*, I need to study. Please, I am leaving. Priety, your book is with me. I forgot it at home. I will bring it *haan.*"

Priety too, tried to make our plan a success "I will come with you. I am going to my aunt's house. She stays near your place."

We quickly left from there, wishing each other luck for the upcoming exams.

Lying to our friends, we got out of the college campus, separately. I messaged Priety to meet me at the taxi stand nearby, following which she arrived 10 minutes after me.

We were already late than our decided schedule "It's 1.30 already…Hurry."

Finding a taxi, we got in, keeping our bags at the window ends so that we could sit close to each other.

The taxi driver put the meter down and asked, *"Kahan jaana hai?"* "Worli…Worli sea face," I said.

We had been to Marine Drive and Girgaum Chowpatty together earlier, but never Worli sea face. The cabbie drove the taxi through Mumbai Central and we reached Worli sea face in around 30 minutes. Throughout the drive, Priety was talking about the exams. She was worried. Actually, both of us were worried as we had hardly studied in the last 5 months. She also handed me the notes she had prepared for the coming exams - Easy and fast to learn! Girls are quite hard working. I was grateful to her.

We reached the place by 2 'o' clock. The sight was awesome. The limitless sea …shimmering in the sun, even though the heat was blistering, the cool wind blowing from the sea felt soothing on the body. The waters were calm today, I realised it was low tide as the rocks, which were usually submerged were visible. There were benches fixed on the roadside, for couples probably. We sat on a bench next the statue of 'The Common man', the creation of author and cartoonist R. K. Laxman.

The thing, I liked most about Worli sea face, was the privacy. It was afternoon and the place was almost deserted. At any given time, Worli Sea face would be less crowded than Marine Drive or Chowpatty. That's why I liked it better. People made the scenic beaches dirty.

"Sashank, aren't you feeling thirsty?" Priety asked.

"No." I said, then realising my mistake in a second, I asked her, "Are you feeling thirsty? Wait, I'll look around for something for us to drink."

I got up and started looking around.

No wonder Jasmine loved Aladdin, because he had the Genie to fulfill the needs instantly.

Luckily, I was saved. My Genie, a little girl, appeared from somewhere. She was a local girl, may be around 10 years of age, selling toys, *gajras*, cold drinks, water bottles etc. Her half naked brother tagged along.

Calling her, I asked, *"Arre…sunno..Maaza dena…ek bottle…kitne ka?"*

Girl *"Sahab..50 Rs."*

It would look cheap, bargaining with this little girl in front of Priety. I quietly bought the cold drink and offered it to her. By the time I looked back, the little girl had disappeared as quickly as she had come.

Priety "Hey Shashank. What is this?"

I tried to be funny in vain "Maaza ... non aerated drink ... *asli aam ka mazaa.*"

Priety "Ohh..no...Maaza, but with a Mirinda cap. Also the seal is open. You should have checked *na*, before buying. Let me check the date of expiry ....hmm..ya its 5/6/2011. (Expressing relief) Still one month left."

I didn't know whether to laugh or cry. I had bought it for her paying Rs 50 for a Rs 25 bottle, and here she was complaining about the cap of the bottle and the seal. Damn it! This wasn't some super market. Why do girls have to mull over everything?

We spent around an hour sitting on the bench speaking to each other. I was beginning to feel uncomfortable sitting on the hard bench for so long, but Priety was busy chattering. I was admiring her and she was pointing out my bad habits. Though I initiated the 'Bad habits' topic, I was at the receiving end. That was because I didn't dare to make any bad remarks, lest she would get angry. But when it was her turn, she came up with a long unending list, after requesting me to have no hard feelings.

I wanted to spend some time with her on the rocks by the sea. So I requested her to visit the rocks with me before leaving, to which she agreed instantly.

I always enjoyed looking at the sea; the cool, humid air, the sound of waves, the salty smell of the sea blowing in the wind there would refresh me. We were walking towards the edge through the uneven rocks. I was walking ahead of her, but could see her from the corner of my eyes. She was still wearing her high-heeled sandals, making it difficult for her to walk freely. Eventually, she slipped on one of the stones. Quickly I grabbed her hand and supported her. Our eyes met and she laughed "Thank you.....Mr. Muscular!" I blushed.

I carried her sandals from there on*. We walked hand in hand, I supporting her as she continued giggling, making fun of me. I felt it was ruining the essence of such a romantic situation. But, I didn't mind. She was with me and she was happy. That was enough for me.

Taking small and firm steps, we reached the place, where the rocks met the sea. We sat on two different rocks.

"Sashank, if people are watching us, they must be thinking we are a couple and have had a fight or something... sitting on two separate rocks!!" she giggled.

I replied with a wry smile. Actually, I hated the fact that we were sitting so far from each other.

After spending some time there watching the sea, birds, rocks, people and all the couples except each other, as if enacting some old Hindi movie song scene, we finally moved out at around 5.15 pm and hired a taxi to our college. On the way, Priety stopped the taxi at Haji Ali. I didn't know what was going on in her mind. We got out of the taxi at the Haji Ali signal.

"What happened, Priety, you want to visit Haji Ali?" I asked, confused.

"Aren't you hungry? Let's go to Sardar restaurant. I love the *pav bhaji* they serve." she said.

The restaurant she was talking about was opposite Hira Panna. I had heard about it a few times from Vicky, so I happily walked towards the restaurant with Priety. Not to mention, I was very hungry as well.

Everyone on the road was looking at us, or so it seemed. I became possessive and protective naturally. A boy was staring at her continuously and walking towards us. As he came near us, he suddenly came nearer to Priety, I gave him a firm push, with an angry look. I guess he understood the reason, that's why he went straight away.

Priety, who was busy talking hadn't noticed the guy walking towards her. "Are you mad? Why are you doing all this unnecessarily?"

Why had I pushed that guy, even I couldn't fathom. I blurted out, "That boy was staring at you. I didn't like."

"Ah… Possessive? I like you Sashank." she said tauntingly.

She held my hand as we entered the Sardar restaurant. We looked for an empty table and found one. After scanning the menu card, we ordered two Amul *pav bhajis*. It took around 15 minutes for the order to come. Meanwhile, Priety was telling me the recipe for *pav bhaji*, testing my patience. I felt hungrier. The aroma of the melted butter on the hot *tava* had set my mouth watering. Even Priety stopped her chatter as soon as beautiful buttered *pav bhaji* arrived. We pounced upon the delicious *pav bhaji* like hungry tigers on their prey. We didn't speak a word until we had finished our respective *pavs*. It was then that I asked her the question that was on my mind, "Do you want an extra *pav*??" The taste was truly superb. It was the most amazing *pav bhaji* I had ever eaten. After finishing, we ordered desert, milkshake with chocolate ice cream topping. We sipped it with the same straw. I was full by the time we finished the milkshake, Priety didn't have much of it and I had to finish it up. The waiter brought the bill and a suggestion slip after sometime. I paid the bill while Priety wrote the suggestions.

Priety, "Sashank, do you have a blank page?"

Me, "Yes…why, you want to take down their recipe?"

Priety, "Give it. Don't ask silly questions."

She wrote something on it, hiding from me. She was smiling while writing. Quickly, she folded the piece of paper and gave it back to me. I was about to open it when she ordered, "Read it when you reach home. Now let's go. It's already late. We need to study."

She has this weird habit of changing the topic immediately.

And then the most wonderful taxi ride began. The taxi moved at a slow speed as there was too much traffic. She held my hand tightly and rested her head on my shoulders. This time it was deliberate. I think the taxi driver understood the tenderness of situation, because he tuned the radio, creating a romantic mood. Luckily, the song was 'Te amo' from the movie 'Dum maaro dum'; one of my favorite numbers. I felt something different was happening in my life, something lovable. I liked my life for a change.

We were about to reach the college gate, when she looked at me with her loving eyes, making me special, on top of the world. The cool air was blowing her hair. She had left her hair open. I could not resist looking into her eyes. We saw each other for a long time silently, no words were exchanged.

Then she held my hand and kissed it and said, "Don't ever leave me. I will never be able to forget you."

She had said those words so easily, I had thought about saying these very words to her a thousand times, but could never muster the courage.

A few strands of her hair were swaying over her face. I arranged them at the back of her ear, all the time looking into her eyes. We were speaking to each other with our eyes. I don't know about her, but I surely was.

Breaking the silence, I whispered "Priety. I ... I ..."

The taxi stopped suddenly. "We are there." the cabbie said, staring at us.

Priety was curious "What were you saying, Sashank?"

"I… I like you and will never forget you." I replied.

I changed my words. 'Like' for 'Love'.

Waving to me, she walked towards her hostel. I instructed the taxi driver to move towards Samson. Even the cabbie looked sad that we had separated, he turned off the radio. I could still see her whenever I closed my eyes, till I reached home.

I rang the doorbell, mom opened the door. I entered; dad was sitting on the sofa, reading a newspaper. I was about to move towards my room, when dad approached me "Sashank, where were you all this time? Your exams are approaching. Don't you know your responsibility? As it is you haven't got a job in the campus placements, I want you to get good marks this time. You must be feeling it yourself, aren't you? Now go study."

I was a little hurt at those words. It wasn't as if I was only one who hadn't got a job in the campus placement round. I hung my head in shame and quietly went to my room, called Vicky and told him to meet me outside my apartment. Friends are a remedy to every problem.

Without telling my parents, I left home.

Vicky and Rahul, "What happened? Why did you call up so late at night?"

I never used to hide anything from my friends "My parents kept on nagging me about the placements *yaar*. So, I was a bit disturbed after such a good day."

Vicky, "Good day! ... Why?"

One has to think ten times before uttering a word before Vicky, he had caught me. "Actually...... after the project submission, Priety and I went to Worli to spend some time together. I am sorry I lied to you."

And you won't believe they weren't angry after listening to this. Actually they were happy that a person from the group was trying to progress in the 'love' field.

Rahul said, "You son of a bitch, we'd have left by ourselves if we had the slightest clue. By the way, did anything happen between you?" He had a wicked look on his face.

"Nothing much, actually. I spent some quality time with her. Some unforgettable memories. You know, I pushed a guy who was gaping at her on the roadside." I said proudly.

"He went from there without even looking back again."

Vicky and Rahul started laughing.

Rahul (in his exaggerated style) "*Bass...Arey yaar. Maarna tha na usko. Balak..tujhe pata nahin prabhu shree Ram ne sita ko bachane ke liye Raavan ka kaise wadh kiya tha.*"

"*Bhai mere.* That was only one Raavan in that era. Nowadays, you'll find a Raavan in every *gali*. How could I fight everyone? And by the way I'm still not sure about me being Ram or Raavan," I retorted.

Vicky, "Haven't you proposed yet?"

"No. By the way, how are the studies going on? Any plans drawn yet?" I asked him to change the topic.

They knew I was changing the topic on purpose. It was a hard habit to lose.

Vicky handed me a bunch of papers, written especially for lazy folks like me; a short booklet enough only to pass the subject. I accepted it eagerly.

After talking, joking, laughing, commenting at each other for about an hour, I went back home.

After dinner, Mr. Sinha summoned me again "Mr. Kapoor told me that he saw you with a girl coming out of our house."

What I had feared had come true, Mr. Kapoor had said everything to dad and also added some of his own *masala*. The truth was that he had seen us in the apartment lobby and not near my flat. But I understood the reason behind Mr. Kapoor's exaggeration.

"Dad, she is my college friend. She had come here for some notes."

- "Does she require the notes every other day? Many other people of the complex have seen you with that girl. Look Sashank, this is the age to study; to build up your career. There are many years after this when you can enjoy. I am sorry for being strict but you won't get any more money from me till your exams get over, then you will understand the value of earning. It is for your betterment. Take five hundred rupees for now. Now, go study."

As always, I was speechless before dad. With a blank face, I went to my room. Dejected, I sat on my bed, and picked up my mobile. There were 12 missed calls from Priety. I was not in a mood to call her. However, some magic made my fingers dial her number.

"Hello. *Kya hua?*" I whispered.

Priety, "Raksheet just called me. I think he is going to propose to me. What should I do now? Should I tell him that I have a boyfriend?"

Raksheet was one of the studious guys in our college who liked her. She was friends with him and had made very good use of his notes. The ones she had given me had also come from him. I didn't know that he was so brave, as to propose her. For every call made by Raksheet to her, a call was made by Priety to me asking for suggestion. She thought of not being rude to Raksheet as his notes had helped us a lot. But after half an hour, she had to break his heart finally.

Priety, "Oh…these boys, I tell you. Raksheet is not of my type at all."

Me, "Ok, Priety … Had I proposed, what would have been your answer?"

I didn't intend to ask but it just slipped out at that moment.

"Hmmm….If I was not in any relationship, I would have surely agreed," she smiled.

With those words, she ended the call.

Suddenly, I remembered the note she had given me at the restaurant. I got my bag quickly and took that note out. The words written on it were …

There I thought I had moved one step ahead from 'Close friend' being her boy friend. Keeping the note in my wallet, I slept.

Next day : 10.30 am

The project had been submitted. It felt as if a burden was off my shoulders. But the final exams were approaching and I was already way behind schedule. I started planning how to go about my studies. The tough subjects were to be dealt with first, the easy ones later. The thinner notes and the most frequently asked questions were my priority.

I finally opened my DTSP notes and started reading the important and frequently asked questions.

My phone rang. *'Kiss me through the phone…'*. It was Priety's call, I had set this ringtone specially for her.

Me, "Hey, Good morning sweetie."

"Good morning, Mr. Possessive. Try to be less possessive mister. It can be dangerous."

- "*Arre aapke liye to jaan haazir hai...*"

Both of us laughed.

Priety, "You know what... Last night, I dreamt of you."

- "Really.. Wow...and what was the scene?"

Priety, "Ummm.... We were a bit close to each other. I mean not too close."

Now I was silent for about a minute, trying to find words to reply.

"Oh. Great...." I replied.

Priety, "What's great in that?"

- "I mean .... It wouldn't make such a good scene if we were sitting far from each other."

"Just kiddin *yaar*. Cool," she chided and started laughing again.

Priety, "Achha Sashank. I have kept a new name for you."

Me, "Achha! Let me also know."

Priety "S2, it stands for Sashank Sinha, and also for 'simple silly' boy. Cool *na*. Now you suggest one for me..."

I had never kept any short name for any girl yet. Yes ... I used to call Rahul 'Tapu' and Vicky 'Kancha' but names like these won't be entertained by Priety. Ok ... let's analyze her name initials. It is PV. The first thing that strikes me after listening the letters 'PV' was *per vaginum'*, that's the effect of reading my dad's books. So, I reversed the letters…VP.

Me "How about VP. VP for very *pyari*…."

Priety "That's so sweet of you. Thank you. And *haan* S2, I am going home today."

"Why, all of a sudden..*kya hua!!* Is everything fine at home?" I asked.

Priety "*Haan re baba*.. Nothing like that. Actually, I wanted to be with my parents for a while and I think I can study better at home, as mom is extra caring during exam days. I am leaving by the 'Deccan Queen' at 5.10 in the evening. I wanted to meet you before going. Will you come to drop me at CST?"

- "But why are you going…we will study together *na*. Who will take care of my studies if you go home like this.."

Priety, "Come on *yaar* S2…*phone diya hai na bhagwan ne*…Don't worry, we will be in contact, and I know you will study well, because you are going to solve all my doubts when I come back. So are you coming or not?...come *na*..please."

- "Yes sure, I am coming."

I quickly closed my books, washed my face and stood before the mirror to comb my hair. The T-shirt and jeans were ok. After a generous spray of the deodorant, I was out of my apartment in 3 minutes. Luckily a taxi was standing right in front of my apartment.

Waving to the taxi driver, I asked him for CST. The taxi driver gave me a typical taxi driver look and nodded. It meant 'Yes'.

Due to heavy traffic, the cab was stuck at the J.J signal for 5 minutes. Meanwhile, I instructed the driver, *"Bhaiyya... Pehle Wilson college ke gate par le lo... Fir wahan se CST.."*

The taxi driver retorted angrily (in Marathi) *"Baghaa saheb. Bhaiyya bolaycha naahin. Me bhaiyya waat to ka tumhala. Me marathi maanus aahes.!!"*

Me *"Achha achha. Sorry kaka. Lavkar chala."*

I was already late, but thanks to the cabbie, the lost time was made up by the time I reached my first stop. I was on time to pick Priety up.

She was standing outside the gate of Wilson College. She was struggling with the zipper of her handbag and seemed to be having trouble in pulling it up. The handbag seemed to be stuffed to the maximum of its capacity, must be her clothes. The only other luggage she was carrying was her college bag, on her back. It looked heavy and I guess, must be full of books. She hunched her shoulders as she walked towards the taxi with her heavy luggage. Today's dressing style was quite simple, might be because she was going home, a simple white *kurta* and plain blue jeans. However, the *kajal* was still there. The hair was tightly tied up into a pony like that of a school girl.

I got out of the taxi immediately to help her. She thanked me and quickly passed on her luggage to me. I pulled up the zipper of the handbag with little difficulty and shoved the bag on the back seat near the door opposite. Then she moved in with the college bag on her lap. I was about to close the door and go for the front seat as I thought it might get cramped for her, with the luggage on one side and myself on the other. But, Priety asked me to sit with her on the back seat. Being a person with an average, I mean a bit more than average body in terms of horizontal size, I adjusted myself on the third seat. It was a bit cramped as I had expected, but I was happy that she was close to me. I kept my hand behind her head for her to rest on. The taxi started.

Me, "Priety, I will miss you *yaar*. Please try to come early…."

Priety, "I'll miss you too. Thanks for coming at such short notice. You are a true friend."

- "Shut up, *Chalo* at least we will be in contact through phone."

Priety, "Hey, I forgot to tell you one thing, we will have to restrict our calls. Mom will ask me a hundred questions if she comes to know about you. Text messages are fine though."

- "As you say, ma'am, but try to call at least once everyday."

Driving through Mohammed Ali road, the taxi stopped at a signal. She closed her eyes resting her head on my arm; I just kept looking at her unblinkingly. It was going to be difficult for me to stay away from her. The taxiwaala, seemingly understanding the gravity of the situation switched on the radio. The song playing was *'In dino dil mera…mujh se hai keh raha…tuuuu…. khwab saja…'* from the film 'Life in a metro'. The song ended with our journey. We had reached CST station. I took out my wallet to pay.

But, Priety held my hand and stopped me from paying.

I tried to protest, but she thrust a hundred rupee note into the taxiwaala's hand.

Priety "It's ok, baba… C'mon let's go now. It's almost 5 pm."

The taxiwaala interrupted. Holding a fifty rupee note in his hand *"Do rupya chhutta dena….Baavan rupya hua."*

I quickly took out a coin from my pocket and gave it to the driver. I felt better; I wasn't used to Priety paying the bills.

We rushed to the platform quickly, after reading the chart. The train had already arrived at platform number 9; departure time was 5.10 pm. I heard the announcer requesting people to board the train with their passes ready for inspection. Her heavy handbag was with me and she was carrying the college bag. Priety seemed a bit lost as to where her berth was. After wasting five minutes running around with the luggage, we finally found her berth.

I gave her some last minute instructions as she made herself comfortable. "Priety… keep an eye on your luggage, robberies in trains have increased nowadays. *Pata chala tere paas books hi nahi rahe padhne ke liye*!! Then surely you'll have to come back to Mumbai na…." I taunted. "Anyways.. I was just joking.. Take care *haan*… Ok then bye. Hope you will come soon."

Priety "Yes, I will take care…thanks for caring about me so much S2…Hey, did you buy your platform ticket??"

She always came up with such absurd questions.

With that question, the train started moving. I got out of the train after assuring her that I would buy the platform ticket. I was standing on the platform, waving. The moving train was increasing the distance between us. We waved goodbye to each other. The Deccan Queen had left.

The next week was like a punishment for me. Throughout the day, I used to study. It was initially tough to spend hours at one place, that too with books and not Priety. However, our messaging was at an all time high. I used to message her and then look at my mobile a hundred times for her reply. Our messages were mostly short sentences which updated our situation in studies … Satcom done, read Wicom from the notes I gave you, DTSP is stupid, I am missing you, me too etc. We easily shared around 50-60 messages daily.

Time flew by and before I could realise, an entire week had passed. The whole week, I was busy reading theory, memorizing formulas, reading up solved examples and then trying to solve some on my own. All of us were bored to death. We sent each other frustrated messages, cursing subjects. The whole week was boring except for one day, when Rahul, I and Vicky went out for dinner, thanks to Vicky's enthusiasm.

Rahul and Vicky met me outside my apartment gate. At eight at night, we stood for a long time, talking about the progress we had made in revision, plans about the remaining days, but after some time the talk shifted to regular topics of discussion like the latest movies, cricket, football and babes. The place for dinner hadn't been decided yet. This is one quality of an all-boys group, all decisions are always instant.

Vicky, "Let's go to 5 Spice."

Rahul and I, "*Chal chalte hai...*"

This one is another quality that there is no arguing on food. Anywhere is fine as long as stomachs are filled.

We got into a taxi. Vicky and I sat on the back seat and Rahul sat next to the driver.

"*Aur Sashank...baaki sab...badhiya??*" Vicky inquired with a smile.

Whenever your best friend asks you that question, it is because he wants to know about the topic that you are hiding from him.

"All's well." I replied trying to keep it short.

Both of us laughed. Rahul was busy watching girls passing by.

"Stop *taapo*fying so hard. Your eyes are already popping out." I mocked Rahul.

Rahul replied, "*Kya kare..* We aren't so lucky to have eyes to dive into and hearts to love at the Worli Seaface. All we can do is *taap*ofy!!" and laughed at his own pathetic sense of humor.

It made me quit the conversation and the other two laughed even more.

We reached 5-Spice. It is a Chinese restaurant near the Asiatic library in the Fort area. We reached there by 8.40 pm. Vicky and I got out of the taxi and walked right into the restaurant deliberately, forcing Rahul to pay the taxi fare. I had my revenge.

Even at 9 pm, we were still on the waiting list. I left Rahul's number at the counter for the receptionist to call us when a table was available. To spend time, we too joined Rahul, whose radar was at full blast as there were many beautiful faces and bodies around. And then the person called loudly "Kancha … Mr. Kancha."

Hearing that unexpected name, Vicky looked at him with a bewildered expression. Rahul and I stood there laughing uncontrollably.

We were still laughing as we sat down. Vicky was fuming. He kept pointing his middle finger at us to show his anger. But then, after a few minutes, he calmed down. This is another benefit of an all boys group. They don't mind jokes or pranks played on each other, *Sab chalta hai.*

It was our ritual to order 'Mission Impossible' first whenever we visited 5-Spice. It's a mountain of chocolate with vanilla ice-cream topping and it is aptly named as it is impossible for one person to finish it. We shared it and after that we ordered dinner. We cursed our subjects, laughed, and passed sarcastic comments at each other as we finished our dinner with great effort. While returning, we were silent. Surely, everyone was thinking about getting back to studies which all of us found boring.

Finally, Rahul broke the silence, "I see us studying to our graves, man. No wonder we are frustrated. I wonder who designed this stupid syllabus."

I bade them goodbye and best of luck for studies and got out of the taxi at my apartment gate. The other two would continue in the same cab till the hostel.

13th May 10.15 pm

Priety usually answered to my messages immediately. If not, at the most in an hour. But today, she hadn't replied to my messages since morning. I was worried. Not able to control myself, I called her up. She didn't take the call either. I logged into Facebook and messaged her. There was no message or update from her that day. Otherwise, she was regular in playing Farmville and Cityville.

Getting worried, I called up Shikha "Shikha. Did you talk to Priety today? She is not taking my call and not replying to my messages either."

"Sashank. Don't you know what happened?" she asked in her usual hyper tone.

Girls can never directly tell us what has happened without exaggerating everything to astronomical proportions.

I asked, "Tell me what happened?"

- "I thought Priety might have told you. She was not answering my call too. It was when I called on her landline number; I got to speak to her. But I didn't expect this to happen...."

I was frustrated by this time and was about to stop this pointless conversation, but I muttered a few abuses under my breath and asked her again,

"Why, what happened?"

- "Priety broke up with her boyfriend. She is very depressed."

Those words were unbelievable for me. I was still doubtful.

I ended the call quickly and dialed Priety's landline number. I prepared myself to talk to anyone who would pick up the phone. I hated myself for having this feeling, but was really glad that it had happened. You see, boys are not angels after all. After about four rings, she picked up the call.

Priety, "Hello."

I recognized her voice, but she sounded a little weak.

I "Priety, Sashank here. How are you? I mean, why are you not replying to my message or call?"

Priety, "I was a bit busy with studies. Mom's calling me for some work. So I have to go."

- "Wait Priety. Shikha told me that you broke up with Hari. Is that true?"

After a little silence for a few seconds, Priety burst into tears. She was crying on the phone. I wanted to be there with her. I could not bear to hear her crying.

Priety, "Yes Sashank. It's true. He ditched me. He told me that he doesn't love me anymore. Seven years ... Sashank, Seven years of trust. All finished in one second."

I could not resist myself from telling her "Priety. Calm down. Everything will be fine. I am coming there tomorrow."

Priety insisted that I should stay in Mumbai. But as I was in love, I was stubborn about my decision.

With some soothing words, I disconnected the call and started surfing for train timings to Pune in the morning. The first train in the morning was Indrayani express at 5.40 am. Getting up early in the morning has always been a problem for me. So, equating the importance for sleep and Priety, I decided to board the Intercity express at 6.45 am.

Now the next challenge before me was to lie convincingly to my parents. Before sleeping, I stood outside their closed bedroom door and spoke in a loud voice "I have to go to college tomorrow and after that I will be going to Vicky's place." Vicky had a spotless image in the eyes of my parents. Love had made me lie again.

Next day 4.50 am

I had set an alarm for 5.00 am. But, I woke up at 4.50. It was still dark outside. I had never seen the environment at this time before. It is so beautiful. With the thought of meeting Priety, I got ready by 5.55 am in a plain white shirt, blue ragged look jeans and my shoes, because Priety always said that men's apparel should be semiformal. That suits men.

I glanced at my watch and realised that it was getting late. I quickly grabbed my wallet. Oh.. the wallet. It was then that I realised that I only had Rs. 632. I thought that was sufficient for today. Dad had got an emergency call in the wee hours of the morning and had just returned. He was sitting on a chair in the hall, having his breakfast. I kept walking towards the door stealthily.

He asked "Where are you going so early? It's only 6 'o' clock."

That moment I realised that I had forgotten to lie about the morning time. My RAM started working faster.

"Some exam related documents are to be submitted. So, the college people have called the students a bit early. After that, we have to attend college too. That's why…"

I quickly rushed out of my house and then out of my apartment. It was already 6.10 am and the train was of 6.45 am. Got into a taxi and there I was at the CST station in 10 minutes as in the morning there is less traffic on the roads. I was hiding myself behind my bag as a precaution. I had to be cautious; I didn't want another complaint about me reaching my dad. After a while, I reached the ticket window and got a general ticket for Pune. I looked at the chart that showed the departure and arrival time of the trains. Intercity express came on platform no. 9. By hard work and a bit of luck, I got a window seat. The compartment got full in hardly 5 minutes. I thought of calling Priety, but then I decided to call her after reaching Pune. I might as well surprise her.

The train started moving within a few minutes. With every halt, the number of people in the compartment increased. I was busy thinking about the ways to surprise Priety and the words to console her, so as to solve her problem and bring that beautiful smile back on her lips.

I was so busy watching the running scenes outside the window that I didn't notice a good looking girl standing near me. I noticed her after some time when I turned to look at some commotion on the neighboring seat. She was good looking, brown eyes, roundish face, straight black hair which was really long and a fair complexion. She was dressed in the purple top and light blue jeans. I thought for a while of offering my seat to her as she looked uncomfortable standing, but then someone got up at Thane station and she got a seat, right opposite me. As she sat, our eyes met, but I avoided looking at her as Priety's thoughts flooded in my mind, she reminded me of my love.

Throughout the journey, I tried not to look at her. But at Lonavla, the girl's leg touched mine.

She said, "Sorry" with a smile.

We both shared a smile. Her smile was indicating something; I couldn't understand it? A small boy came and sat on her lap calling her "*Didi didi.*" Then a man standing at the door confirmed that the boy had reached her by asking from the door itself. Probably, he was their dad.

The little boy told to his sister that he wanted to sit on my seat so that he could feel the breeze. She tried to quieten him, but he was adamant. On hearing the conversation, I had a smile on my face. She looked at me and smiled back. I asked the little boy if he wanted to sit on my lap. Initially, he refused but agreed later after I offered him a chocolate. Within 5 minutes, the little boy dozed off on my lap. On seeing that, the girl offered to take him back, but I assured her that I was comfortable. Then our conversation started. I got to know that she was a medical student, studying at GMC, Mumbai and was on her way, visiting her relatives in Pune. Her name was Duaa Khan. She was a final year student, like me. We shared some of our funny college experiences from our totally opposite fields. It was great talking to her and we had almost become friends by the time we reached Pune. We then shook hands and took leave of each other.

I was feeling a bit lost in Pune. It had been a long time since I had last come here. It was around 10 am by the time I got out of the train with my college bag and walked out of the station to the rickshaw stand nearby.

Pune had changed a lot since I had last seen it. Flyovers, subways, buildings, wide roads, new restaurants all seemed very attractive. Pune looked like a metropolitan city now. Just as I was standing at the rickshaw stand, preparing myself to surprise Priety and meet her, it started raining. I think it was the first shower of the season, everyone seemed happy. People were rushing here and there for shelter as most of them were without umbrellas. The wind had started blowing hard; all of a sudden it became pitch dark. It seemed as if a thunderstorm was approaching.

I always liked the smell of the wet earth after the first rains. Different people have different thoughts about rain. I remember writing poems, sitting on my balcony.

My favorite one goes like this -

Seasons change, moments never

It is not the rain that makes you smile

It is the memories that stay forever.

But today, I had a different thought regarding rain. It was

With the thunder, lightning and children seeking shelter.

People call it as the season of rain.

Today, the drop of water seemed to me like God's tears

As if even God was feeling her pain.

I called her. "Priety. I am in Pune. Can you please meet me somewhere? I want to talk to you."

- "Oh Sashank. Why did you ... I mean ...are you really here ...ok, meet me opposite Marz-o-rin at M.G.road. I will be there in 20 minutes, *paagal*."

Standing on the roadside with the drizzle still continuing, I was thinking of the way to M.G road as I was totally confused about the directions she had given me. But, I didn't want the rickshaw guys to know that. So, with some false confidence, I called a rickshaw.

I doubted its brakes, because it went away without even noticing me. But, as people say "When you don't get something in life, it is because God has planned something better for you."

Then came a totally new, swanky rickshaw. It looked like a vehicle for an amusement ride. Colourfully decorated, with a music player playing a song which I couldn't even understand... not only I but anyone outside the rickshaw wouldn't be able to make head or tail of it, as all that one could hear outside the rickshaw was the thumping bass effect. That's what you call a 'Rickshaw DJ'. The basic colour of the rickshaw was black and yellow. But, every attempt was made to hide the black colour by drawing colorful flowers on it. In the front, next to the light was written 'Jai' on one side and 'Maharashtra' on the other side, in Marathi. There was a small red flag attached to rickshaw. The driver stopped the rickshaw a little away from me as he applied the brakes firmly. The auto screeched to a halt, it was almost a 'Rajni' style stunt. As I was approaching to sit in the rickshaw, I saw something absurd written at the back of rickshaw. It was a printed sticker that quoted 'Don't spit. Stop AIDS.'

Now, it was hard for me to believe that. I went a bit closer to it and saw that two stickers had got overlapped with the 'Stop TB' part got torn from one of them. I smiled to myself. As if that wasn't enough, there was another sticker above the red lights at the back. It was …

"*Surakshit antar theva, nahi tar aat yaa*". That meant, "Keep safe distance, or else come in."

Now, that was a real innovative line. Where do these people get these innovative lines from? I then remembered that it was a speciality of the city. One could come across numerous such lines outside buildings and shops, even when one went out for a stroll.

I went to the driver to ask him for M.G Road. Meanwhile, the music was still going on. He was not able to hear me. So, I told him to stop the player with sign language. With an annoying look, he stopped it.

I asked, "Will you take me to M.G Road?"

The driver was just a young boy, probably too young to get a driver's licence. He was dressed flamboyantly with a shining red shirt over white trousers, a few gold chains dangled from his neck and he wore a superman T-shirt inside. He was a thin dark skinned fellow, a typical *gavwala*.

Driver "Ya sure, why not...but the fare will be 25 rupees."

I looked at the meter. It had been converted into a showpiece with an image of thumbs down printed over it. That meant, 'Meter down'. Now that was another innovative masterpiece. I agreed immediately and got in.

With the great pick-up, ride started. Sitting at the rear seat, I was worried as I could see that the driver was able to see only partly through the windshield, because most of the windshield area was covered by a variety of things. One third of the top was covered by idols and photographs of gods and goddesses such as Lord Ganpati, Lord Shiva, Lakshmi and in that list was a picture of Sachin tendulkar too. In the lower section, he had fixed a wooden drawer, containing compartments for the music player and I don't know what else. It seemed as if he was playing some racing game on play station. On the right side next to rear view mirror, he had kept a handkerchief, that too of bright colours, next to the sticker of *'Shubh laabh'*. While driving, he took that handkerchief and started wiping the sweat looking in the rear view mirror. It was then I noticed that on the sticker not only said *'Shubh laabh'*, but, it was *'Shubh laabh mala hou de'*. I smiled. The driver was one of a kind. He was sitting on one half of the seat with one leg straightened to rest outside the rickshaw.

I was so busy in exploring this unique guy and his vehicle that I didn't notice how time passed and reached M.G Road.

M.G Road seemed to be the most happening place in Pune. There were people everywhere. It looked like a site which could almost match the Hill road at Bandra. The branded outlets everywhere were full of people young and old. People walking around were fashionably dressed in trendy outfits. I liked that place. But for now, after the amazing ride, my next aim was to find Marz-o-rin.

Marz-o-rin is a famous place on M.G Road, so I didn't have to struggle to find it. I stood opposite the place for about 10 minutes till Priety arrived. Her eyes were looking different, swollen with dark circles around them. She looked weak. That showed her grief, but I was happy to see her after such a long time.

"Hey. How are you?" I asked.

- "I am fine now. Come. Let's sit inside."

We both went to the restaurant. Today, she was trying to be a bit distant from me. I could judge her state of mind from her silence.

We entered Marz-o-rin. It is one of the most famous snack corners in Pune. I read outside that it was started in 1965. The place is famous for its pastries, bakery products, juices, milkshake … those too in affordable prices. The ambience is beautiful. This place gives you an old world feeling with wooden chairs, wooden tables, ancient looking lanterns on the wall, wooden flooring that sound of timber as you walk by. The whole atmosphere was cozy.

Scanning through the menu card, I ordered a Mac carina chicken and mocha for me and a Multigrain chicken roll and coffee for Priety.

Breaking the silence I said, "Priety. I can't see you like this. I can't see you sad. Please say something."

Without warning, Priety started crying. She was sobbing quite loudly. Tears started rolling down her cheeks. Everyone sitting there stared at us. I am sure they thought that I was guilty in some way.

I moved my chair near hers and tried calming her down holding her hand and giving the people nearby an innocent look to save myself.

"Priety. Please calm down."

The same moment the waiter came with the things ordered. Even he gave me an annoying look.

A few more minutes passed silently. Unused to this kind of silence I started the conversation directly regarding the break-up as I was eager to know what exactly had happened.

"Priety, what happened between you and Hari?"

Priety gulped her coffee and began, "Break-up ... 7 years of relationship broken in a second."

- "I am sorry to interfere. But, if you want you can share with me the details, what exactly happened."

Priety continued, "Hari came back from Bangalore three days back. He had been away for three months and had been very busy. We hardly got time to talk to each other in that period. I was very happy to meet him. We were sitting at Barista. I took his mobile and started watching his images. There were about 10-12 images of Hari with a girl. On my asking, he explained that she was his colleague in summer internship. I didn't ask for any explanation further. But, when he took my mobile, he got angry watching my photos with you, the ones at Worli and after that he went on to read your messages, then the messages I had sent to you. He got furious and started shouting at me in front of all the people sitting there. I controlled myself and kept silent. I tried a lot to convince him. But he turned a deaf ear to my words. Then I got angry and started questioning him about the pics in his mobile. As if waiting for the opportunity, he said that we could not stay together any more.

I stopped and stood up when he used the words 'Break-up'. All the memories, the happy moments, the fights, the time we spent together, the late night phone calls ... everything flashed before my eyes in that second. Throwing me out of his life, he stood and started walking away. I still hoped that he would come back. But, he didn't even turn back."

Listening to that, I felt sad. I couldn't bear to see her in that state. Even my eyes became wet.

With a heavy heart, I said, "Priety. Don't worry. We will find some way out."

- "No Sashank. Though late, I have understood that Hari is not the person that I want to stay with for the rest of my life. I am happy that this happened, it's just that the memories keep coming back."

I could see the anger on her face. But, with her great ability, the smile camouflaged the anger again.

Priety, "Ok. So how's Pune? And how's the delicious food in Pune? Did you like it?"

Helping her to forget the break-up, I exaggerated that the food was great. Personally, I didn't think much of the food.

And we both laughed. I was happy to see that smile again on her face.

Evening 4.00 pm

We spent hours at Marz-o-rin and then walked on the M.G Road. She was back to the way she used to be with me. The laughter was back. Everything seemed to be going on well.

She said "Hey S2, now I will go home. I have to pack my bag. I am going to Mumbai by the 6.45 Indrayani Express in the evening. Are you planning to stay here or go back tonight? If planning to go, then we will go together."

I was flabbergasted to hear that plan. I hadn't booked my ticket yet.

I said, "What the hell are you talking about. You are leaving for Mumbai, then what is the point in my staying here, of course I am coming with you!!"

We decided to meet at the station entry by 6.15pm and then she left for home. It feels really nice to make someone happy, especially to someone who is very special to you.

I came back to the Pune station, relaxed. Still lost in her thought, I was walking on the platform with the earphones plugged playing some romantic songs. My stomach was full and still there were 2 hours left for the train to arrive. I needed to do something to pass the time. I called up Vicky.

"Vicky. How's study going on? Done with studies?"

Vicky replied, "Haha. That's a funny question. You know me. My preparation is always incomplete. Only God can save me now. By the way, you are studying, right?"

I didn't want to tell Vicky that I was in Pune but the announcer at the station had already started. While I was answering Vicky's question, there was an announcement "Intercity express is arriving at platform number 4." Vicky heard that announcement on the phone.

Vicky, "Where are you? Are you on a railway platform?"

It was never easy to lie to Vicky, so I told him the truth ... half-truth.

- "Yes. I am at CST station. I came here to see off my relatives."

Vicky's brain works like Sherlock Holmes.

Vicky, "It's not possible. I heard the announcement of Intercity express. It leaves Mumbai in the morning, not in the evening. Sashank ... are you in Pune? Don't lie to me... *saale.*"

I thought there was no point in lying to him further. So, I gave in. I told him about Preity's break up and how I had to come to Pune to console her.

Vicky, "See Sashank. I might sound rude. Priety had been close to many boys of our college in the past. She has played mind games with many people in the past. You know Raksheet... He is not the one who will propose just any girl he meets. He will propose only when a girl will take a step forward to get close to him. He met me some days back. He told me how he used to meet Priety outside college campus, go for movies, restaurants, every evening and when he proposed her, she rejected even his friendship.

Now, Raksheet is so depressed. Look, I am not saying that Priety is a bad girl. But, don't get too involved. And also the exams are from 16ᵗʰ. You need to think about the exams first. Think from the brain, not your heart. Ok?"

I never got angry at Vicky's suggestions. "Ok Vicky. I get it. But it's true that I love her. I can't help it *yaar*." I justified.

Vicky replied, "Ok now. You come here. After the exams, we will speak about it. And please study. I want all three of us to graduate together. 'The three engineers'…!! " I hated his joke.

With those words, Vicky disconnected the call. Vicky's words made me think about the whole situation again. Was I acting foolishly? What was I doing here wasting the whole day when I should be studying; the exams were just two days away. I started having a mild headache. I decided to think about that topic later and checked my watch. It was 5.20 pm. I decided to buy the tickets. So, I went to the ticket window and bought two tickets for Mumbai. At around 6.20 pm, Priety came to station.

She apologised profusely, "Sorry Sashank, I got a bit late, couldn't get an auto in time. I will go and buy the ticket. Will you wait here with the luggage please?"

"Wait. I've bought the tickets. Take this." I smiled.

"Keep it with you. You take good care of things." she said patting my cheek.

With those words and her smile, Vicky's words got washed off from my brain as if they were never there.

There was an announcement, "The Indrayani Express is arriving at platform number 4..."

We rushed through the foot over bridge quickly to platform number 4. Priety decided to sit with me instead of sitting in the ladies compartment. I was happy at seeing that affection for me back in her eyes. Though I respected Vicky's words, I still thought Priety the most beautiful, kindhearted and honest girl.

An aged couple was sitting on the seat in front of us. They had got their seats after a long struggle and after settling down with their luggage, the old lady heaved a sigh of relief and rested her head on her husband's shoulder. I smiled at seeing that but Priety didn't, she became pensive. Her eyes filled up with tears but she didn't let them fall.

With a sudden jerk, the train started. As the train's speed increased, the words of Priety's talk too gained momentum. She has a talent of covering each and every random topic in one conversation. You need to have a lot of patience because she doesn't let you talk. After some time, the old couple too joined in our talks. They were jolly people. Time passed by swiftly and we reached Lonavla. At Lonavla, many *vada pav* vendors, people selling soft drinks, groundnut sellers and many more passed by, but Priety wasn't interested at all in having that. But, when the jelly seller came, her desire to have it was like a small child.I asked the vendor to give me a box of jellies. Preity interrupted and asked specifically for the green ones.

I sheepishly asked, "Why only green?"

I knew I had committed a mistake right then. Preity replied, "Green is my favorite color. But how would you remember that? You would never bother, would you? Anyways, you can have your separate box of jelly"

I looked at her and then at the aged couple opposite us. I was not that experienced to respond quickly to such a situation. The aged couple tried to explain a lot about what to do at such situations, with their gestures. But, I was not able to solve the mystery. When this attempt of the aged couple failed, they tried a new method.

Uncle told aunty, "Roopa, what is your favourite outfit? Please."

Taking their clues, I built up my confidence and bang came my question.

"What's your favorite subject, Preity?"

- "What! Favorite subject! Subjects are not to be liked Sashank."

That was quick. Once again I wasn't prepared for the situation. They looked disappointed. It was then that I realised that even a trained donkey can't run like a horse.

I changed my question quickly, "Which is your favourite movie?"

- "*Jaani dushman.* That too in 3D." and she laughed. The old couple joined in the laughter. Till now, I was used to her weird sense of humour. With such countless moments, the journey continued.

Night 10.10 pm

Priety was sleeping with her head resting on my shoulder and I slept with my head resting over her head. The uncle sitting in front of us woke us when the train reached CST. I took charge of our luggage, I mean Priety's luggage. We were just moving out of the train when the old couple approached us smilingly. They wished us luck for our married life. That took us completely by surprise, but we really liked them and thanked them awkwardly so as not to dampen their enthusiasm.

We bade them goodbye before leaving. They waved back at us and walked away, hand in hand.

We then looked at each other for an awkward moment and then burst out laughing as we moved towards the exit.

Throughout the drive from CST station to the college gate, we were laughing at the old couple's comments. Just as there are always some speed breakers on long smooth roads, there were study related concerns, which acted as speed breakers in our long smooth conversation.

At the college gate, I asked her, "Hey VP, the luggage is too heavy. If you want, I can come till your hostel gate."

But she refused. I don't know why. I didn't want to think about it. I wished her good night and left for home.

Next morning 15th May 10.10 am.

Yesterday had been quite a memorable day for me. The journey to Pune, Priety's tears and then her happy face, Vicky's call too and finally the narrow escape from dad's questioning at home.

Today was the day to study, I decided. The practical exams, beginning tomorrow, were scheduled to be over by 21st May with not much gap in between exams. The first practicals were of WiCom. I took my books and notes out to study the circuits and the basics. After studying for two hours, my brain was saturated. So I got up, stretched myself and decided that it was time to relax. I relaxed, listening to music. It was after about 40 minutes, when I realised that I had wasted a lot of time, so I quickly switched off the music player and got back to studies. After lunch, I studied till the evening without any break. In the evening, I felt like having tea. But there was nobody at home to prepare it for me. So, I got up, made some tea and was back with my books. Wicom is an interesting topic. That's why, I was able to read it and grasp it quickly. I had covered more than half the portion by evening. At around eight in the evening, mom came home and was happy to see me studying. I knew it was indeed a rare sight for my parents.

I had a brief chat with my mother and told her that my exam was scheduled at 12.30 the next day. Mom gave me dinner in 30 minutes as she had promised. I finished my food quickly and went back to study. For the first time in life, I was feeling a change in me regarding the sincerity towards studies. It's unbelievable, but for the next 3 hours I studied without any break. I was feeling sleepy. The doorbell rang. It was my dad. I was weary after studying the whole day, but still I continued. Dad came to my room after having his dinner and getting fresh. Even, he wished me luck for the exams and told me to get some rest before sleeping. It felt good.

It was around 2.30 in the night. With much effort, I got up and switched off my the lights in my room. I took my cell and messaged Priety.

Best of luck fr tmrw VP

I got a reply instantly.

Thnks....Best of luck 2 u 2. Really S2...we need the luck a lot!! gn

Then I slept setting an alarm of 9 am.

Next day 10.30 am

"Tring tring ... tring tring" that was my alarm tone. It was irritating me for a long time, and finally I got up. A feeling of doom crept over me as I saw the clock. The poor thing had been ringing continuously for the last one and a half hours. But, my ability to sleep was greater than the alarm because it was 10.30 am, the time when I usually woke up. I quickly rushed to bathroom, had a bath and had breakfast that my mom had prepared before leaving.

The time was 11.15 am. I grabbed my notes and started going through them briskly. I was multitasking - wearing shoes, packing bag, reading notes ... all at the same time. When I was about to leave, I remembered that dad had kept the car keys on the table for me. Dad was not that bad, during exam time. Happily, I thanked him in my mind; took those keys, locked home and went towards the lift. Really, during exams, even the time spent in the lift, the lobby or the car is precious. Getting into the car, I kept the notes next to my seat.

I always enjoyed driving Dad's i20 but today, I did not have time to experience it. I was in a hurry. Though I tried a lot, it was impossible to stop myself from enjoying the ride, the smooth steering, great interiors, A.C and all, everything was rich. I felt almost out of place in that car, my wallet was almost empty.

I stopped my car at the signal near J.J. Hospital. It was 3 minutes left for the signal to turn green. I took out a pen from the pocket of my shirt and started reading the notes underlining the important points. I don't know what the point was in underlining just 45 minutes before the exam. But it helped me to remember those points.

7

16TH MAY – 1ST JUNE
JAVED'S VERSION

I decided to accept Aadesh's advice. I was ready with the duplicate key to Sashank's locker. The only task left was to notify Dinesh, Santosh and Toya about this. With mixed emotions of anger and guilt, I suppressed the voice of my conscience and decided to go ahead with the plan.

Evening 8 pm

I was still sitting in my corner on the footpath when I suddenly realised that it was getting dark and I hadn't had a morsel of food since my morning *chai bun maska*. So I got up to search for some place to eat.

It's really tough to search for anything when your brain is already busy looking for something else. To divert my mind I fooled myself into being philosophical and speaking to myself.

Mumbai is a place where nobody stays hungry and it takes care of your personal tastes too. Whether the person rich or poor, he will surely find something to satisfy his palate. It caters to the youth with a taste for the latest multinational cuisines as well to the oldies with its Parsi hotels with their old world charm, reminding us of an era gone by. Really, it is a typical example of the sentence – Unity in diversity, I had read in one of my schoolbooks. However, that was written to describe our nation.

With these vague thoughts in mind, I stopped suddenly as I saw a signboard on a hotel. The letter 'A' seemed to be disowned by the shop owner, as it was devoid of the beautiful fluorescent light and the higher status that the other letters of the word enjoyed. This was the National Restaurant, I entered and took a seat.

"*Ae chhotu. Chal phadka maar*, and quickly bring a plate full of hot *kheema* and four *pavs*. Before that, tell someone to give water. What *seth*! Teach them some manners." I said.

Nowadays, I don't feel important to scan through the menu card before ordering a dish, as I am least worried about the cost. I had started earning well enough. I tried the well maintained, posh hotels. But, I didn't like the taste there. It's simple logic - the taste of *kheema pav* is far superior to chicken burger.

As I was very hungry, I almost gobbled the dinner. Then I squeezed a quarter piece of lemon into a glass of water, drank it, paid the bill,

116

kept the change on the plate and stepped out of the restaurant to walk towards my place.

Saala, Mumbai was getting hotter day by day. The heat was enough to hinder my sleep at night and during the day, I was drenched in sweat. But, these rich women never looked sweaty as we did, I wondered how they managed, it must be the make up I thought.

I was just two minutes away from Samsun apartment, when Dinesh and the other three met me.

Aadesh, "What Javed, *Kidhar?* Had dinner?"

I said, "Ya, Just had it."

Dinesh, "*Arey*. Let's go to Hotel Banjaara. Today we will drink vodka."

"No no. I don't drink." I disagreed.

Dinesh, "C'mon. We got a good amount at Ghatkopar. So, just to celebrate, please accompany us."

Still disagreeing, I said, "*Nai yaar,* you go and enjoy yourselves."

Aadesh, "What Javed! Only this time…ok, just taste it. You never party with us."

Santosh, "Yes Javed. We were doing minor work before you joined us. You are the one who changed our lives and made us richer. Thank you Javed."

Suddenly, Aadesh started laughing and just controlling his laughter, he stood right in front of us and said, "Hey you people. Do you know, soon, our Javed is going to be a much richer person. A rich *saab*, that too, with a *memsaab*."

Toya, "Why? Whath happennth? Whooth yol *memtaab,* Taved?"

"You will get to know after a while. First, you all just take an oath to help Javed fulfill his dream," Aadesh placed a hand over his heart.

Everyone agreed with Aadesh without a second thought.

Santosh, "Yes, brother. He is our friend. Now, will you explain the matter to us?"

Aadesh pointed his finger towards Samsung apartment and said, "You see this apartment?"

The rest nodded to Aadesh's idiosyncrasies.

Aadesh, "In this apartment, lives a boy. He is very rich. But, he has committed a mistake. He is sharing an unexplained relationship with Javed's signal girl. Bloody Bastard."

I was fuming with every word.

He continued, "Just make up your minds that we have to rob him. And please, don't get tense about the keys. That work is already done by Javed. So, what do all of you have to say?"

Listening to that, the other three walked to me, Santosh said, "Javed, don't worry at all. We will surely make this plan a success. And be at ease, your name will not figure anywhere in the plan. That girl is yours and yours only."

Toya, "Yeth Taved. Gal will be youl."

Next day 17th may 5.15 pm

"The success of any robbery depends on the way it is planned. Planning is a must." Aadesh had said. He has been the mastermind of the robberies done till date.

Santosh, "So Aadesh. What's the plan?"

Aadesh, "Listen friends, before planning anything, I need to get some information. Information about that boy, about the members in his house….When do they go out, when they come back, the watchman, his work timings ... anything important. For that, we need to keep an eye on them for the next 5 days and then on 22nd, after analysing the situation, I will prepare a plan. Is that ok?"

Dinesh, "All that is fine. But brother, it will be easy for us if you can tell us, precisely, what we have to do."

That statement brought a smile to our faces. I was beginning to wonder if I'm the only one clueless in the group.

Aadesh, "Ok. Toya, you will gather information about the watchman. When does he come for duty? When does he leave? Where he stays...everything.

Santosh, look for the guy...no no let it be. You go to the guy's place in pizza delivery boy's disguise, at around 9 to 10 pm, and look for the number of people in the house and give me their daily schedule.

Dinesh, go into the apartment in the disguise of a municipal anti-mosquito gas blower. As soon as you get into the building, start with fumigation. That's all."

The last sentence baffled all of us, especially Dinesh.

Dinesh, "What! I have to do just that!!"

Scratching my head, I was trying to make sense of Aadesh's words.

He broke the silence with his laughter, "Oh Dinesh, did you take that seriously? Oh man, after getting into the building, you have to get information about every nook and corner there."

Dinesh, Santosh and Toya, "And you? What will you do?"

Toya was the one whose voice was heard clearly amongst the chorus, but though Toya lisps, his intention can be guessed easily by his facial expressions.

To that, Aadesh replied, "I will be arranging for the bike and the other minor things that will be required."

"And what about me? What should I do Aadesh *bhai*?" I asked.

Aadesh, "Just sit and dream. Arey Javed, just relax. Don't get into all these things. We are there to care of everything."

For the next four days, the robbers…oops, my friends were busy with their job, the job allotted to them by Aadesh, the job to make my dreams, a reality.

My eagerness didn't let me realise how those four days passed; the eagerness to experience the moment of success and feel happy.

22nd May 8 pm

According to Aadesh, today was the day of finalising the plan. They were expected to come any time now. But, they had not turned up yet. They were already half an hour late. My eyes were looking for their faces in the evening crowd. Eventually I gave up and sat down at my place, rubbing my tired eyes.

Who says man cannot see after closing his eyes? The fact is, as soon as one closes his eyes, he moves aloof from the surrounding humdrum and his mind sees what he desires at that very moment

As soon as I was immersed in my thoughts, Aadesh patted my back and said, "*Kya* Javed bhai, lost in dreams? Wait for some time..let the moon rise at least. Haha….Or else wait for some days..then there will be no need to dream with open eyes…it will all be there for you…in reality."

Aadesh could make anyone happy with his sweet words.

Smiling, I said, "No *yaar*, I was just a bit tired. By the way, why are you people so late? I waited for you for so long."

Santosh, "*Arey* yaar. It took time to arrange the bike."

I, "But, you people could use the pizza delivery bike which Santosh used the other day for getting to the boy's house. Couldn't you?"

Santosh, "No no, not at all. That bike had its number written over it, and was borrowed from some *chhokra* nearby. If we use that bike, it will be easy for the police to nab us. That's why we arranged another bike from Mulund's second hand bike market, fixed the pizza box on it, very low so as to hide the number and painted it to give it a look of pizza bike."

Toya, "Whath Thantoth, you couth have lemoveth the numbal plathe."

Santosh, at his persuasive beat, "Toya *beta*. Don't take tension. I mean, don't get stressed for such silly things, we, your well wishers, are there to handle it. Big animals don't use their small brains."

Toya, annoyed, "Whath!"

Aadesh, quickly interrupted, "Toya, he meant..aa..he meant big animals. Haan...as you know we all humans are actually animals, living animals, and as you are a strong bigger man, that's why a big animal. So, a big animal should not use their...their brains for such small things. They should be used on more important occasions."

Somehow managing such a lengthy explanation, Aadesh gave Santosh a grim look, which Santosh ignored by saying, "Let's discuss the plan now."

Aadesh, "Ok? Did you people do your job properly?"

I was fed up watching them argue on irrelevant topics. So, I raised my voice to stop them and asked Toya to initiate the talk with his information.

Toya, "Thel aal two wathman. They wolk fol twelve houlth eath. One of them ith Lameth (Ramesh). He liveth in maathgaon. He wolkth flom seven in the evening. Fol the nekth twelve houlth, Tturreth (Suresh) wolkth. He thayth at kulla (Kurla), comth by tlain.

Both aal vely puncthual. Both aal vely thin too, will geth down in juth one fighth."

Aadesh "That will not be needed, Toya. And Dinesh, what about you?"

Dinesh "My friend, after blowing gas from that big heavy gunlike thing, I started feeling as if I was Arnold Schwarzenegger of *The Terminator*. It was so hazy out there, that it was impossible to see anything. But, when I came down from the top floor, the gas was totally gone. I saw that there is only one way for the entry and exit of the building. There is a lift and it works really fast. The boy stays on the sixth floor, third apartment on the left as we step out of the lift. The number of the flat is 213. To get out of the complex, there is only one way, from the main gate, as the compound wall is around seven feet high on all four sides."

Aadesh "And you? Please speak up, Mr.Santosh."

Santosh "Ya sure. I went there with the pizza bike, disguise and all. I wasn't looking at all like a pizza boy, but like a pizza uncle. The watchman inquired what I wanted, but I handled the situation well and managed to get to room no. 213. The time was 9.30 pm. There was a man, a woman and a boy at home. The boy and the woman were in casual attire. But, the man seemed to have arrived just then, as he was in his office formals, resting with his legs on the lone table in the room. And yes, before I forget, I saw a maid too. She just came after I reached. After observing them for the next three days, I came to the conclusion that the maid comes daily at 9 pm. The boy's parents are both doctors. His father leaves at 8 am daily, and reaches his hospital at Ghatkopar, in a taxi. There is no fixed time of his return.... 9, 10, 11, 12...but never before 9 pm. His mother leaves by nine in the morning for her Colaba clinic, and returns at 8 pm sharp. The boy leaves for his college at 11.30 am daily in his white i20 and a returns home by 4 pm and is at home after that."

Aadesh "Good work. So now, everybody listen carefully

Toya, you will be following Suresh the watchman right from Kurla. You will board the same train with him and then in the train you will have a heated argument with him. Do it on any topic... be it a push, or abusive word...anything. The objective is to make him reach the apartment late by at least 45 minutes.

Dinesh, as soon as Ramesh leaves his place, you get into the building pretending to be a courier. Put on an artificial beard and moustache to camouflage your face. And this is your bag, a few letters."

Aadesh took out one letter from the bag, with 'Confidential' written over it.

Aadesh "Dinesh, this is the letter for Mr.Sinha. If the watchman asks anything or tells you to drop it there at the entry counter itself, tell him that the letter is confidential and it needs to be handed to the concerned person. And yes, this is the 'received' letter, on which you need to take the signature of that boy. By 7.10 pm, you should enter the building.

"Santosh, you become a pizza boy once again. This time with a helmet and the glares too. You should be reaching the building lobby by 7.15 p.m."

"But keep this in mind, Santosh and Dinesh, there should be a gap of at least 5 minutes between your entries in the complex, and by 7.20 pm, both of you should have reached the boy's apartment. First, Santosh will ring the bell and deliver the pizza. At the same moment, Dinesh will ask the boy to sign the 'received' letter, after handling him the letter. With the pizza in one hand and the letter in other, the idiot will surely go towards the table kept in the hall, to keep the pizza on it. That is the moment when both of you have to barge in, tie the hands and feet of the boy and stuff his mouth with a cloth. Wasting no time, you then go to the locker, open it; empty its contents into the courier bag. First, take all the jewellery, then go for the cash. All this should be done latest by 7.45 pm. After that, quickly leave the house, close the door, get on to the pizza bike and empty the courier bag into the pizza box. Just take care, nobody sees you doing that and then get out of the apartment, separately, one after another. Just remember, the boy's mother reaches home by 8.00 pm; that's why you don't have much time to waste."

"And Toya, when Suresh leaves after the quarrel, you will call Dinesh and inform him.

When the whole episode ends, Santosh, you ride to our place in Colaba.

Dinesh, you reach by bus, and don't remove your disguise before you reach Lamington Road."

Dinesh, "Lamington Road? Why would I go there?"

Aadesh, "You will go Lamington Road first, and from there you will reach Colaba by another bus. So, with your normal face you will go to Colaba.

Any doubt anyone?"

Everyone stood, with a new found respect for Aadesh's intelligence.

"Aadesh, wouldn't you be part of this job?" I asked.

Aadesh, "No *yaar*. It won't be possible for me. Exams are approaching and I want to pass B.A, unlike these three, who keep on failing year after year. Listen, knowledge brings respect." The knowledgeable *pravachan* was interrupted by the ring of Aadesh's mobile. He looked for a minute at it and then went a few steps away from us to attend to the call. He was looking very happy, while speaking on his cell phone; surely it must be someone special.

I said to Dinesh, "I think Aadesh's speaking to his mom. He is looking very happy."

Dinesh laughed at me and said, "Not possible, might be one of his 'items'. Our Aadesh is a hero. He has many girlfriends. When there is a call from his home, he hardly speaks for even two minutes."

After listening to that, my faith in Aadesh became more stubborn. I thought he was the right person to direct me, to get that girl in my life.

Aadesh was busy on the call for at least half an hour, after which he came with the smile still there on his face. "So, guys, let's have a banquet to celebrate the commencement of our objective."

Dinesh, " Oh … banquet! Just see what words he is using … banquet. All because of the conversation he had with the girl, just now."

Aadesh, "Haha. Let's go."

We all left to go to the Shimla restaurant. Tipsy Bar was on the way. There I saw that the same Samsun apartment guy was very drunk, so much that he was unable to walk steadily without his friend's support. We stood there watching our future victim.

Aadesh, "Javed, See him? Today, he is enjoying his life. But, he is unaware that in few days, he is gonna lose money, and his girl. Then he will be drinking deep in sorrow and we will celebrate."

We both laughed.

For the next week, the plan occupied our brains. I was very happy and grateful to get the company of such friends, who were helping me fulfill my dream. If they hadn't met me, my dream would have remained… well, just a dream, and a dejected awakening. But, it was because of them, especially Aadesh that my dream was turning out to be a reality.

In the meeting on Sunday 29th May, we came to know that the boy's schedule had changed. He used to leave his flat by 10 in the morning and would return by 2 in the afternoon. However, this didn't affect our plan.

Every member of our group was just waiting for the final day…1ˢᵗ June. Toya, Dinesh, Santosh, Aadesh and I too were worried about the plan. But yes, Aadesh had some extra tensions too…of his mother, exams and most important of all, tension of his girlfriends, because whenever we all met, he was busy on the mobile. I too wanted to be like Aadesh.

1ˢᵗ June 6.00 pm

As per my regular schedule, I was standing at my key stall on the footpath, but was busy watching Samson Apartment. The moment to perform the task, as decided was fast approaching. The parents of the boy hadn't reached home yet. Ramesh the watchman was seated on his chair at the gate. As expected, the boy… I means that idiot, had already arrived.

I was scared, I don't know why?

The weather was also acting a bit different. It seemed that it would rain, that too heavily. A cool air was trying to bring down my temperature which had risen, the result of being over anxious. To add to this, the thunders were loud enough to send a sudden shiver through me. It got dark by 6.15 pm. As soon as it was 7 on the clock, Ramesh stood up and within 5 minutes was back, with his clothes changed. He was continuously trying to call someone; I guessed he might be trying to call Suresh. He gave up in a while and started walking towards the bus stop nearby. In a few seconds, he boarded a bus to Mazgaon and left.

By 7.10 pm, Dinesh came there, as a courier man. At first sight, I did not recognise him; the bag he carried helped me to recognise him. His moustache and beard were very bushy, but the shape was like that of Amitabh Bachhan's beard. He was dressed in ironed clothes with a cap on his head. When he did not see anybody at the entry gate, he went inside, walking suddenly at a faster pace.

Somebody entered the gate on the pizza bike by 7.15 pm. He might be Santosh; I could not see his face through the helmet.

Time was moving slowly. I was sweating heavily, despite knowing that I did not have any role in this robbery, not directly at least. When this was not enough to increase the tempo of my heartbeat, something absurd happened; Suresh the watchman came there by 7.30 pm.

I was flummoxed. How could he reach so early? Didn't Toya do his job properly? What would happen now? Should I go and distract him? How will these people move out? What if the boy created problems? Were Dinesh and Santosh caught? My head was swarming with innumerable possibilities.

Suresh casually walked to his chair, swinging his hands, giving the impression of trying to swim through air. He then sat down on his chair, completely unaware of what was going on flat number 213. Even I was unaware.

It was already 7.40 pm, and they were still inside. The time for the boy's mother to come was approaching. Where the hell were these people? Meanwhile, the watchman had made himself comfortable on his chair, sitting with one leg on the chair seat and the other spread out.

A hundred thoughts were passing my brain. But, in the next 5 minutes, I saw something that made me dizzy. From the Samson apartment gate came Dinesh. He was at ease. I felt alive, watching him after waiting for so long. Every minute feels like an hour at such a moment. Dinesh did a thumbs-up from far, indicating that the job was done.

I just started heaving a sigh of relief, when I saw Santosh coming out through the gate on the pizza bike. But, instead of feeling happy, I felt as if somebody plugged a live wire of 1000 volts into me, because I saw Santosh seated on the back seat. Yes, Santosh was not alone on the bike; the same guy whom they had gone to rob was seated on the front seat, riding the bike.

Where did he come from? What had happened? I was totally confused. Unable to think of anything, I just stared at them, open-mouthed.

In a flash, they rode towards Mohmd. Ali Road. I stood there analysing this short suspense drama, suddenly I rose from my limbo, quickly packed up my tools and left for Colaba.

Their hub in Colaba is located at a remote place behind the

government chawl. One has to go through many small lanes and diversions to reach it.

I had heard the proverb - 'An idle mind is the devil's workshop.'

This idle place was like a workshop for these modern day devils.

I reached there, avoiding anyone's eyes, and knocked on the door. Dinesh opened it after a few seconds. He held my shirt collar and pulled me inside. When I got inside, it was hard for me to breathe, as the room was very smelly. I saw that Santosh and Dinesh were standing there facing the boy, who was lying on the floor.

I asked Santosh, "Why the hell did you bring him with you?"

My question was interrupted by the boy, as he asked Dinesh, "Who is he, your boss?"

Dinesh, "Javed. Why did you come here? You should have kept yourself away from all this."

Me, "*Yaar*, watching all that drama, I was so tense that I couldn't stop myself from coming here."

Suddenly, Dinesh got frustrated with anger "*Saala*, Toya ruined the whole plan. He failed to do his job, that too at such a crucial time. Now, the whole plan has got reversed."

Seeing Dinesh being tense, the boy quickly stood up and said confidently, "Hey you guys, don't worry. Nothing will happen to you… "

"Just follow my plan, do as I say."

8

16TH MAY - 1ST JUNE
SASHANK'S VERSION

Today was the first viva, the journey through hell was about to start; the subject was WiCom. Though not a difficult subject, as people say, the viva had always been a problem for me.

I was worried about reaching late, so I drove the car quickly to college. The mindset of a student is totally changed during exams. It is exam time when a student gives God, absolute respect. He prays at every worshiping place and sometimes even at the old sculptured Parsi bakeries, by mistake. Driving through the lanes, passing signals and avoiding potholes, I reached the examination room by 12.20 pm. The practical was about to start. My roll number was in the middle of the lot, which always saved me from getting late.

I was ready for the viva with a lot of confidence and a little bit of knowledge. Students moved one by one, as their turn approached for getting slaughtered, although some scholars had an extraordinary desire to impress the examiner, there were many like me who loved to live…happily. I preferred to go with the flow, not expecting anything great to happen. I always entered the room like a general who has lost and come for ceasefire. People coming out of the room often looked like unsuccessful doctors coming out of the operation theatre, dejected with heads down. But, even after watching so many victims, there was no drop in enthusiasm of the remainder… enthusiasm to know the frequently asked questions.

Finally, the college peon, who seemed to be enjoying himself, called "Roll. no. 163." Hearing that, a wave of thrill passed through me and I stood up from my chair, wiping the sweat with my handkerchief, walked two steps ahead, and sat down on the chair, which had just been vacated by Avinash, as he stood after hearing his roll number.

I wished him, "Avinash, best of luck."

Avinash, "Thank you."

I always avoided studying at the last minute, because that confuses me and brings my confidence level down. I was trying to calm myself, when I saw a friend of mine, Unzer reading something which looked alien to me, "What is this, where was this?"

Unzer, "This is Prof. Parulekar's notes, a favorite of the examiner. Don't tell me you haven't read this."

I didn't want to tell him the truth, so I said, "No no, I had read it, just the font size is different and that's why I got confused."

It was then that the devil's messenger came once again, "Roll.no 164."

I entered the room, and within 15 minutes, my viva was over. Please don't ask me what was asked. I won't be able to answer that, because I didn't even remember the questions, as I had heard them for the first time in my life.

With such horrifying experiences, the vivas came one after another, and the days passed. Though I frustrated the examiners many times, I was blessed with some good vivas too; the best amongst them was SatCom and Radar. The examiner asked me the mechanism and circuit. Thank God, I answered them well....a student thanks God for each and every small thing that happened in his favor during the exams. This keeps him happy.

Though I tried hard to concentrate on my studies, it was customary to share 'best of lucks' and 'good nights' with Priety. But, I succeeded restricting the calls and chatting to give more time to studies.

21st May 4.00 pm

Today was the last practical, Internet communications. It was good..actually ok. But, I was sure that I would not flunk. As soon as my practical exam was over and I got some free space away from friends, I called Priety "Hey Priety.. Hi, how was your practical?"

Priety, "Fine.. actually *itna achha bhi nahin tha.* How was yours?"

I said, "Struggled as always. But, I handled it. Thank God. By the way, could we meet at Delhi Darbar for dinner tonight?.. Or if you are busy studying for theory, it's ok. We'll meet after the theory exams. What say?"

Priety, "*Yaar,* I'm sooo frustrated studying for practicals. I will meet you at DD at 8 pm. Be ready to have some delicious Butter chicken. Bye."

Ending the call, I quickly drove home. I had a smile on my face throughout the journey. I loved the way she said "bye". The car's loudspeaker volume was at maximum level. Life felt much lighter, I reached my apartment in about five minutes as all signals were green, parked the car in the basement and went home.

Sleep was the only thing I desperately needed as I had got the least of it in the last few days. So, I undressed quickly, cleared the clutter of books on my bed, enough to make space for myself and was asleep in no time.

That night 8.15 pm

Buzz….buzzzzz..the noise woke me up from my anaesthetic sleep. Somebody was at the door ringing the bell. I opened the door. It was mom.

Mom "What Sashank! Where were you? It's been ten minutes that I have been ringing the bell. And where's your mobile. I also tried calling you."

Me "I was sleeping, mom."

With those words, I realised that mom had arrived home. That meant it surely was later than 8.00 p.m. I went quickly to my room to look for my mobile. After searching for few precious minutes, I found it and saw that the time was 8.18 pm and the screen displayed eight missed calls and five messages from Priety. All messages inquired my present location.

I got ready quickly and rushed out of the house in no time. Being late, I was worried about Priety being alone at Delhi Darbar. But as soon as I reached there, my worry turned to surprise, as Priety was not alone this time. She had come with her friend Aasha. It was tough for me to avoid noticing Aasha. She was one of the best looking...I mean sensuous looking girl in our college. She had been a close friend to many geeks of our college. Some said that it was because she believed in social service. The innovative experts of our college had given her the title *'Aasha...garibon ki Bipasha'*. But *yaar*, she was hot.

But when I saw Priety standing next to Aasha, my steps slowed down as I started searching for the reasons to explain the delay. Priety gave me a cold stare. I think, appreciating Aasha before Priety, made her more angry. However, as per Newton's first law of motion, I finally stopped before Priety.

"Where were you? Where do you keep your cell? Silent mode as always *na.. ?*" a rapid-fire from Priety.

"Umm…err..I was sleeping," I said.

Priety, "What! Now, sleep is more important than me for you *haan.*"

I said, "Actually, I was sleeping and was not willing to wake up as you were in my dream."

Girls like such stupid reasons, they feel that *apnapan*. It worked for me. Priety's anger disappeared in a second and then tilting her head a bit down with a shy smile, she reminded me of Aasha's presence with her eyes.

That smile was the start of a beautiful evening followed by mouth watering Butter Chicken, Paneer Jalfrazi, Chicken leg Biryani and smooth buttered Missi rotis and Kulchas. The dessert, was the favorite of all three of us… Caramel Custard.

I finished earlier than the two girls. I had actually forgotten all table manners and had come down upon the sumptuous delicacies, wielding the knife and fork like two swords and myself as some brave knight battling with his enemies, in this case dead, flightless birds. And rightly, the buttons of my trouser were a bit stressed. So, after waiting for some time, I excused myself, stood up and walked to the washbasin, washed and wiped my hands and then took out my wallet. I was standing some two steps behind Priety and Aasha, both seated on chairs. And then I experienced the most embarrassing moment of my life. Searching from various angles, I found that there were only 10 Rs in my wallet. At that moment, truly from my heart, I cursed my dad for stopping my pocket money. I got worried about paying the bill, which was noticed by Priety as she inquired raising her eyebrows. I told her about my condition in a silent way so that Aasha wouldn't know. Doing that, I kept the wallet back in my pocket. Aasha and Priety stood and went towards the washbasin.

I just sat on the couch, thinking of ways to tackle the situation when the waiter came with the bill. I saw Priety and Aasha returning to the table. I took the bill, went through it and acted as if taking out my wallet, after checking my back pocket 2-3 times "Oh... oh shit. I forgot my wallet at my home. *Yaar, kaisa hun main bhi.*" I had to lie to save my face.

I had been a fool to not check my wallet before leaving home and now had to resort to this drama, I hated every moment of it. Avoiding eye contact, I waited desperately for their response.

Priety said mockingly, "*Haan tum to aise hi ho*, It's ok, we will pay the bill, *kitna hua?*"

I was not in a position to refuse them, so I agreed.

As we moved out of the restaurant, I told Priety, "I will pay both of you in college *haan*. Sorry..and thanks for not sending me to clean up the dishes."

Priety smiled and said, "It's ok *yaar*. We are friends. No need to thank and all."

Hearing that, I thought of sharing with Priety, the fact that dad was angry with me because he had seen both of us together and that he had stopped my pocket money for the same reason.

Priety noticed that I was thinking of something, "What happened Sashank, what's the matter? If you want, you can tell me."

In a whispering voice, so that Aasha couldn't hear, I said, "Priety, my neighbors had seen both of us together a few times and they told my parents. Dad was very angry with me; he has put restrictions on me and stopped my pocket money too."

Priety, "Oh ok, calm down. Everything will be fine with time." She had placed her hand on my shoulder, "..and you owe me Rs. 250..!"

That night 11.30 pm

After finishing the satisfying yet embarrassing dinner, I dropped Priety at her hostel and went home, walking.

I was welcomed in the usual way at my place, the same cold vibe which I could feel even as I entered; sharp words were being exchanged between mom and dad. At first I thought it was coming home so late at my exam time that had made them angry. Mom looked at me with angry eyes and stomped off to the bedroom while dad sat in his corner, with a glass in his hand, going over some papers. A few seconds later, I realised that it was the same 25 year old war which I had interrupted. 'Dysfunctional' was an adjective that could have perfectly described my family. They could barely stand each other, even at the best of times and my presence or absence hardly mattered.

Over the years, the sound and fury between them had decreased but they were yet to come to terms with one another. I often wondered how they could be so insensitive towards each other, especially when both of them were doctors. Maybe they had drained all their sensitivities on their patients and when it came to each other or me for that matter, they didn't have much left. They had subconsciously played a role in me getting into engineering and not medicine. I was forced to take science after 10th and then after 12th there were only two options, of which one I would not have chosen at any cost, so engineering chose itself. However, I had grown to like the field. Machines were good, they never doubted you, and they worked as well as you could make them to, as long as you wanted them to, no complaints or grudges. And apart from all that, engineering had given me Priety. I had something beautiful and soothing to look forward to now. All other thoughts evaporated from my mind the instant I thought of her. She was my solace. Damn, I loved her.

I knew I had it coming for me today as I was late, without permission and that was an offence in my house. Somehow I managed to sneak into the sanctity of my room, barely dodging the verbal volleys coming from the bedroom as well as the living room. Most of them were directed towards me, some towards each other and others to no one in particular and everybody in general. Bruised, though largely unscathed, I entered my bathroom directly and turned on the shower at 'full' so as to drown out their voices in the sound of running water. It was such a sudden change in scenario, from the warmth and love of Priety to the emptiness and hatred in my own household. I couldn't digest it and by the time I entered my room, I almost had tears in my eyes. I longed to be with her again.

The long time spent under the shower had freshened me up considerably, so much so that I sat down to study straightaway. The practicals were dealt with somehow but the real test would be during the theory exams. The practicals can be managed with some self confidence and last minute studying but the written exams demanded a lot of study hours to be put in. I started preparing a study time-table so as to make maximum utilization of the available time before the written exams, which were scheduled from 23rd May to 1st June. However, after spending almost half an hour on that, I realized that I was wasting time already and it would be best to start with my studies right away. Time-tables never helped anyone.

So, I opened my books and sat for some time. However the words were out of focus, I was not able to concentrate at all. The memories of the recently spent moments with Priety just kept coming back, wave after wave. All I could think was of her. Feeling fatigued, I lay down on my couch for some rest.

Suddenly my cell phone sprang to life and started vibrating violently. It was Vicky's call, "Hey, where are you man? There's a party at Muni's place!!"

I had heard that name for the first time, "Muni…Who's Muni??"

- "He was our batchmate *yaar*, in first year. Even I don't know him personally, but I do remember that he had sponsored our cricket kit back then, and tonight there's a party at his place and everyone's invited. *Bade baap ka aulaad hai..*"

"How did you come to know about this party?" I asked.

- "Shikha called, and yes, Priety's gonna be there too, so stop interrogating me and get ready quickly."

I almost jumped at his words. Priety had not said anything about any party. Trying to sound calm, I replied, "Okay, but still.. lemme see.. the condition at my place is like a volcano that has just erupted.."

Vicky, "Ok, call me back about your status, *jaldi.*"

"Ya sure."

As soon as I ended that call, Priety called, "Hey S2, are you free?"

"Yes.. I'm coming for Muni's party.." I complied with her even without hearing her question. But that was her magic, I couldn't have read her mind if she hadn't given me the key to that lock.

"Oh, you already know about the party, then why didn't you tell me?"

Girls have the license to ask such unanswerable questions

"*Yaar,* I was just dialing your number when you called.."

Priety "Okie, anyways, so when you leaving?"

All obstacles had disappeared "Be ready in 10 minutes. I'll pick you up at the college gate. See ya." Now even if the whole world tried to stop me from going to the party, I would beat them to it.

In some 7 and half minutes I marched out of my room, fully loaded for the party, in my multicolored party uniform, hair gelled up, symbolizing helmet, badges though not metallic, but printed on my shirt, my belt resembling a bullet case. Holding my shotgun viz. my mobile and large woodland shoes, I stood in front of my dad with the expression of a soldier who stands in front his general before going to war.

Dad looked at me with a sordid expression. Not letting my confidence fizzle out, I said, "A friend of mine is throwing a party. Everyone is going, me too. Will be a little late." I couldn't complete my sentence as I was cut off by dad's booming voice, "And you are telling me now, you don't even bother to take your fathers permission?"

I was about to say "No", really…. believe me, when mom arrived at the scene. "Why does he need your permission when he has mine." turned to me, "Go *beta.*" And again at dad, "Don't put unnecessary restrictions on my child."

Analyzing the situation, I stepped closer to mom; it also helped as she was standing closer to the doorway. That very moment dad stood up in anger, "Pratiksha, don't interfere."

Mom, "What interfere? He is my child too. Go *beta* go."

Looking at mom and dad up in arms once again, I sneaked out of the house, quickly entered the lift, was out of the building and into a taxi in a wink. I called Priety, "I've got a taxi, will reach college soon. You be there at the gate. Ok bye."

I laughed to myself, remembering how mom had saved me. Their fight had helped me, for once.

The taxi took a final turn and entered the straight lane leading to our college. Priety was standing there waiting for me. She hadn't noticed me and was looking at every passing taxi and then at her cell phone as if searching for something. It was when I halted a few steps away from her that she noticed me, waved to me with a smile and approached the taxi.

She was wearing a black, sleeveless, V neck mini dress that stopped a good few inches short of her knees. The neckline of her dress was tantalizingly deep; it was complemented with a large, fancy, black leather belt which she wore above her waist. Her silky brown hair was let loose and was shining in the dim light of the street lamp.

She was looking stunning. It took me some time to adjust to that vision of beauty as I just sat in the taxi and ogled at her, my reflexes had slowed down and by the time I extended a slow hand to open the opposite door, she had already opened it. My extended hand brushed her neck as she entered. She sat next to me, looked at me with a questioning smile "What??"

I shut my open mouth and stammered "Umm..em. nothing..you are looking gorgeous."

She gushed, narrowed her eyebrows and almost shyly said "Sashank...stop it."

I couldn't take my eyes off her. She was wearing black stilettos, with numerous laces winding above her ankle, over her shapely legs, a grey colored multi wrap cuff bracelet around her wrist and was carrying a shiny dark grey clutch on which a large gem shone proudly.

The beauty of a girl's eyes gets multiplied by infinity when enhanced by *kajal* or eye liner. I could lose myself in those eyes. I could have almost imagined it was my heart beating out of its skin but realised in a few seconds that it was my cell vibrating. It was Vicky calling. I had completely forgotten informing Vicky that I was going with Priety and now it was too late. Priety had already arrived.

"*Arre* Vicky..sorry."

Vicky, "Where are you?"

"I'm about to reach Muni's house."

Vicky, "*Waah beta*..so you have finally learnt lying to friends. Look towards the college gate."

I was confused, I looked at my mobile and then towards the college gate. Rahul and Vicky were standing there, waiting for a taxi. As soon as our eyes met, I was speechless with guilt.

Priety had just made herself comfortable besides me and was saying something to which I turned a deaf ear.

The call was still on "*Chal yaar*, don't worry, I ain't angry with you. A girl can't come between our friendship. Meet me directly at Muni's place when you get free. We will come by another cab."

Meanwhile, Priety was busy telling the cabbie some address of Napean sea road, which I suppose was Muni's. Priety's comfort and the concern for my friends were conflicting in my mind. I was in a dilemma of sorts.

The taxi had just started, I put a hand on the cabbie's shoulder, "Just a minute, *bhai saab*. Stop the cab."

Priety, "What happened, you forgot something?"

Hesitatingly, I said, "Vicky and Rahul are standing there for a cab, I can't leave them alone."

I got out of the taxi. Both of them were still standing there, trying to get a taxi. That can sometimes be a difficult business in Mumbai, getting a taxi. I had been lucky that day.

I waved at them, "Rahul, Vicky...come...!!"

I could see a smile on Vicky's face as he approached. They were about to reach when Priety asked, "But Sashank, where will they sit?"

That question hurt me a little bit. A taxi per se, is meant for four people, if you minus the comfort. I could understand her hesitance but this was a trivial matter.

Rahul didn't know about Priety sitting on the back seat. He rushed towards the taxi, walking at a faster pace than Vicky, atypical of him and suddenly halted on opening the door, stared at Priety for a second, and then uttered an unexpected "Hi". It was reciprocated by Priety in an even more surprised tone. Rahul had opened the door on the opposite side and Priety was surely not prepared to sit between me and him, I could read that in her "Hi", it meant, "What are you doing here you fool, leave us alone!" I quietly guided Rahul to the front seat, an intelligent decision as I knew his size paralleled mine. But Vicky was barely affected by her presence; he gave me a smile and entered.

Wasting no time, as we were already late, Vicky and I adjusted ourselves on the back seat, I being in the middle. Throughout the drive, I was busy trying to pacify her, that too without speaking a word. I knew she would be cranky, this sort of behavior is almost unacceptable to girls, but I hoped she would understand, they were friends. I noticed that she had tied up her hair. Some people say that a beautiful girl looks even more so when angry, I found that to be true. And well, talking about the rest, they were busy talking to each other, making guesses about the party.

It was quite late by now, but the roads on both sides of the divider were still full of cars moving through Girgaum Chowpatty and Walkeshwar, we reached Muni's house, in no time.

The venue of the party was a colossal two-storeyed mansion and the party, it seemed, had already begun. Priety moved out quickly and joined a group of girls of our batch as soon as the taxi stopped. She didn't even look at me, she was really angry. I kept my eyes on her as she greeted and hugged her friends in the typical 'not so real' girly fashion, blowing air kisses and all. Meanwhile, Vicky and Rahul were busy gawking at the place and keeping an eagle eye over the girls in our class. Everyone seemed different....more attractive. Everyone had a tough time with their practs and this was a great occasion to unwind. Priety had moved into the mansion with her friends. I was feeling a bit neglected. She was behaving as if I wasn't there.

The three of us entered and after the usual wavings and greetings and handshakes and hugs, I settled down to a place near the stairs in the corner. Guys and girls were busy eating starters and drinking; drinking wine, whisky, rum and soft drinks too. I think Muni's parents were very liberal to allow him to have a party with drink. Even people whom I considered abstemious, were seen standing in the queue for liquor. Rahul was busy chatting with an athletic looking guy, who I suppose was Muni, as he stood at the door, welcoming people. He caught my glance and waved at me with a big smile. I also smiled and waved back. Surely, event management might have been a better option for him.

I wasn't able to see Vicky in the crowd. But that didn't concern me as my eyes were looking for Priety. Eventually, I found her sitting with the same group, near the bar counter. I waved at her; she looked at me for a second and then continued with her smiling and talking with her friends. I was feeling like an ass sitting there, doing nothing.

Suddenly, Muni went to the DJ table and took hold of the mike "Good evening, guys and gals, my friends and friends of friends, welcome all. Hope you all are having a great time. I hate to see everyone huddled up in groups. C'mon love birds. I invite all couples on the dance floor. Let's have some music. Cheers."

And slowly but surely the love birds came onto the dance floor and into each other's arms. The music started and the dance floor was filling up quickly. It was the laziest and most irritating tune I had ever heard, and stayed the same throughout the dance, giving no clue of its termination. I stood watching Priety as she politely declined guys asking her for a dance.

I realised it was high time for me to take some initiative. But having had almost no previous experience, I didn't know how to go about it. Gathering some courage, I left my place and walked towards Priety and stood at a little distance from her. Surely, she had noticed me. But still she wasn't talking to me. I overheard her friend Aasha asking her the reason for her refusal to dance. She looked at me and then turned towards Aasha and spoke loud enough for me to hear "I am still waiting for someone special to ask me."

I had got my signal. I walked towards Priety, held her hand, looked into her eyes, and asked "Priety, will you dance with me?"

She looked at me for a moment, I held my breath. Then, she smiled and placed her hand over mine with a smile, approvingly. It was then I realized that the tune wasn't that bad...actually it was perfect. I felt as if the tune filled love potion everywhere, making everything so romantic. We were dancing, close to each other.

While we were doing slow steps, I saw happy faces all around. To my surprise, even Rahul was capering around with his partner......Aasha. Vicky was also enjoying himself with his partner.......alcohol. Being in each others arms, we were enjoying every moment of it. She looked like an angel, her hair, now untied again, rustled over my right hand which rested on her back. I held her hand firmly, while her left hand rested over my shoulder. We were so engrossed in dancing that we didn't even realise when the others had stopped. It was when they all started clapping for us, we acknowledged that. Any other girl would have felt shy, but Priety was not any other girl; she bowed and told me to do the same, we then thanked everyone by waving to them. I liked this *bindaas* attitude of her.

Dancing was a great form of exercise, I realised. And all the carbohydrates that I had gained from the sumptuous Delhi Darbar meal, a few hours back, had been burnt out. I was feeling famished. In fact, we both were very hungry and straight away headed for some food. People were continuously approaching us and paying compliments, as we ate to our fill. My trouser was beginning to get a bit tight round the waist again. That was the signal. I kept my plate aside and headed to get some ice cream for myself and Priety.

Just then there was an announcement by Muni. It was about playing hide and seek, but it was with a twist, couples were to hide and seek together. I was in no mood in playing games with a heavy stomach, but Priety seemed excited about it, so I had to give in. Some 15-20 couples had joined in. Thankfully we had to hide. The job of seeking had gone to another couple, and I could imagine what the boy might be feeling. Poor guy, he didn't seem pleased.

We had some 30 seconds to hide and rushed to find a safe place. Muni's residence was an opulent two-storeyed bungalow that had many rooms, making it easier for such a large crowd to play the game.

Priety and I entered one of those rooms, but weren't able to find an empty place. From under the bed, behind door, gallery to bathrooms, every place was occupied. We finally got a place where we hid ourselves….the wooden wardrobe. It was filled with clothes with a small free space, where we somehow filled ourselves. The width was just to accommodate a person. We were inside such a congested place to hide. She leaned on the wardrobe sidewall and I stood near her, with hardly any space between us. We were breathing heavily after running around. Our breaths sounded even more laborious in the closed wardrobe, it was an audible sound in the silence. We were trying to calm down, when somebody walked in the room. Priety quickly controlled her breath and kept her hand softly over my mouth. Standing with a girl so beautiful with practically no distance between, with the girl keeping a hand on mouth and looking into eyes unblinkingly, any boy would feel as I did, like making love to her.

I initiated by moving closer to her, keeping both hands on the sidewall that she was resting on. I held her hand which was over my mouth and kissed it. She looked at me longingly with her loving eyes, her lower lip twitched nervously. I moved further, intending to kiss her. She knew that, but she didn't turn her head and kept watching me. I stopped when her lips were a centimeter from mine, my hands were slipping downwards below her waist, but she quickly leaned back, not allowing any more space for my hands to explore, then she pulled me towards her, and our quivering lips met. Softly and carefully, we planted short kisses on each other with pauses in between, each time she was watching my eyes and lips before kissing with a different desire. But then I held her by her waist and pressed her lips firmly over mine, our lips squeezed each other passionately; they seemed to be locked into each other for ever. Strands of her hair were all over my face, I brushed them aside and continued kissing her, then I moved down from her lips to the side of her neck, she reacted as if an ice cube had touched her neck. She gasped as I kissed her neck more and more fervently. I was losing control over myself now, I pulled her dress off her shoulder and kissed her shoulder, my hands pulled her dress further downwards and I started fondling her breast. Priety, who was completely involved in the act till now, suddenly pushed me away and pulled up her dress. But then, she came close to me and again started kissing me, I complied.

We were both at the peak of our emotions. I slipped my right hand down her waist over her mini dress, slowly moving my hand over the soft fabric. I was searching for the touch of her skin. There I thought, I was hiding and seeking at the same time. As I approached the hemline of her dress, invariably my hand slipped inside to feel her. I felt a rush of adrenaline as I touched her thigh. She was having goose bumps which I could feel as I moved my fingers over her skin. Involuntarily, I tried to pull up her dress.

Suddenly someone started banging on the wardrobe door. Initially it was like a soft tap on the door but the sound became progressively louder, till it was a deafening thud. But we were least bothered and continued to kiss, with the same fervor. But then, I heard a familiar voice calling my name "Sashank…Sashank." I suddenly stopped. Priety stopped too, and looked at me with a blank expression. I recognised the voice, and was horrified, it was my dad. How could he be here at this point of time, and how could he know where I was hiding… something was wrong, I had started sweating profusely and was feeling uneasy. I closed my eyes for a moment. Then the door of the wardrobe opened. Yes, it was dad indeed. He looked at me with a confused sort of expression. I was feeling ashamed and barely managed to meet his eyes. "Why are you sweating so much?? Switch on the air conditioner *na*.. go and sleep on your bed, and what is this mess, clear up your books and sleep after that. Good night."

I was dazed. Preity had vanished from my arms, the wardrobe had vanished too. I looked around for a moment. I was lying on my couch in my own little room. Fuck, it had been a dream! I woke up to see dad leaving my room and me sitting on my couch. I was still sweating. What a dream that was! If only I could have such a dream every night. I smiled to myself.

I was alone in my room laughing at myself. I could remember each and every moment of it clearly. Me, standing up against dad, and mom coming forward to support me, I should have realised it was a dream back then. It could only be a dream. But the last part of it was just, enthralling. It was actually like having sex. In fact, I was having an erection when dad woke me up. That was partly why I was feeling ashamed.

Preity's thoughts occupied my mind all the time. She had saved me from embarrassment at DD and man, she was looking so beautiful. But she was something else in the dream, she had an angel like aura around her in my dream, I could feel the affection in her eyes, her talk, and her touch.

I started talking to myself, "Hari must be really insane to break-up with her. But, thanks to him, she is single again. Yeah, she is single now."

That thought set my pulse racing.

The talk with myself started again, "Should I propose to her now? What if she rejects me? And what if she feels hurt? No no, why would she? I love her and she loves me...mostly *toh*."

It took me around half an hour to solve the hassle in my mind, whether to call Priety or not. Finally I called. She picked up at the second ring; I was still not sure what I was going to say.

"Hello Priety, were you sleeping?"

Priety, "No, *Par kya hua. Is samay call kiya.*"

With fear, more than confidence in my voice, "Actually ... I wanted to share something with you."

Priety, "*Kya hua.* Dad scolded you again. Or started your pocket money" she laughed.

"Haha. No *yaar*. The pocket money issue will take some time to get solved. I wanted to say something personal, something special." I said.

Priety, "Tell *na*, please."

Wasting no time, I spoke up.

"Priety. From the first day we met, I have always liked you. I like your eyes, your smile, your talk, your presence, your soul and I want to be with you forever. Priety.................. I love you."

I stopped with those words, awaiting her response.

Priety, "Sashank, I considered you my best friend. Why did you have to say this? Just because I spent some time with you doesn't necessarily mean that I want to be with you forever. Why can't a boy and a girl just be friends? Sashank, you just ruined our relationship. You knew I had just broken up with Hari. You must be waiting for this opportunity *na..* And for your kind information, I still love Hari, and I don't love you. I want my man to be independent, not someone who is dependent on his parents for everything. Did you hear that, I don't love you and now I don't think you are a person worth my friendship too. Good bye."

My heart was crushed after hearing that. Priety's words were unbelievable for me. I called her again and again. She rejected my calls initially, but I kept on trying. Finally, she switched off her cell phone.

I was shattered. Where had I gone wrong? After all that had happened between us in the last few weeks, what else was I supposed to feel? Had I been just a crying shoulder for her? I couldn't understand. It was hard for me to accept the truth that Priety was not my friend anymore. My head was throbbing with pain as I was too stressed.

I was inept to analyze the situation. Priety's words kept ringing in my ears, not letting me sleep. That was the first night I felt that my eyes were wet.

Next day 22nd May 5.00 pm

Last night had been a nightmare for me. I was ashamed of my deed. I tried apologizing to Priety. But, every attempt was a failure. She rejected my calls, warned me not to call her and even barred my messages.

The desperation to apologise to Priety was hard to defy. I was feeling lonely. So, I called Vicky, "Vicky. Meet me at Tipsy bar."

Vicky, "What happened? You are sounding different, actually weak."

Me, "Nothing. Just reach there in half an hour."

Tipsy is a hot spot in Umer khadi for frustrated people. It's a bar cum restaurant. Its perfect dim lighting creates an ambience that has a soothing effect on you. Also, in the dim light you can't see the outside world that had hurt you. Vicky met me in 20 minutes. We went inside.

Me, "Vicky *yaar*, nothing seems right. What should I do?"

Vicky, "*Saale..* First tell me, what happened."

Me, "Ok, but promise you won't tell anybody."

Vicky stared at me for a second and then, "No no not at all. I will tell everyone, will publish the matter over Facebook. Rascal, you still fail to trust me, after being best friends for so many years. Go to hell, if you want to, tell it or else I have no interest. It's that girl, isn't it??"

Me, "No *yaar*, it's not like that. Last night, I called Priety and proposed to her, and she rejected my proposal. *Bahut sunaya mujhe.*"

- "*Iski maa ki..... Kya bola usne.*"

Me, "Shh, you please don't get angry. It is my fault, I misunderstood her friendship."

Vicky, "See Sashank, I warned you about this earlier. Now listen, don't ruin your life like Dev.D."

Me, "Dev.D?"

Vicky, "*Abey...Devdas.*"

Me, "No buddy, she is my life. I can't live without her."

Vicky, "Stop saying that nonsense. You know, girls are like buses. If one goes, another comes. So, don't worry. And by the way, it's good that this happened; Priety was not a good option at all."

Me, "Vicky stop. She is a nice girl. I proposed to her. So, I was at fault."

Vicky, "Let it be *haan*, proposing to a girl whom you have dated a thousand times, is not a crime."

Me, "No buddy. *Chal chhod.* What will you have? I will have vodka."

Vicky, still in an angry mood "*Kuch bhi.*"

I did not usually drink more than two 60 ml pegs. That was my upper limit, after which it was impossible for me even to walk straight. And Vicky too, never took more than a quarter during our regular get togethers. But now, I desperately needed a higher dose, so I ordered, "Three quarters of Smirnoff, one Fanta and one Limca."

Vicky, being a veteran at this game, stopped me and changed the order from three bottles to two and said, "Don't ever get emotional on such topics. Now, please forget that whole issue, and enjoy the moment."

We sat there silently watching people, drinking the golden aqueous, making wavy movements on the tune being played, and their eyes reddened. After some time, the waiter approached with a large platter, kept two empty glasses, a bowl full of peanuts, two glasses of colorless vodka and the cold drinks, on our table. The waiter then poured the fluids into our glasses, in the typical courteous way, while we were busy eating peanuts.

After everything was done, Vicky and I raised our glasses to make that tinkling sound and said "Cheers" to start off. I had decided to put his words to practice, but didn't succeed at first. However, after a few sips things seemed to lighten up a bit.

For the first two pegs, we made some intellectual talk about studies, funny incidents from the past, but after that, our talk progressively became senseless. After finishing one quarter each, which consisted of two bottoms-ups, the difference between our capabilities became apparent; I had become totally ataxic, and Vicky still was able to nod his head within the perfect predetermined limits. After finishing the leftover vodka, as golden top, I wanted some more, so I started singing, *"Humka peeni hai, peeni hai, peeni, peeni hai."*

But, Vicky didn't allow me, "No Sashank, we have to study now. Remember, tomorrow is our exam."

However, I persisted, *"Humka peeni hai, peeni hai."*

- "No, no more drinking."

In a singsong tone, I said, "Who said - I want - to drink - more - I want - to pee - *Humka pee - ni hai, pee - ni hai, pee - ni hai."*

Vicky closed his eyes in frustration for a minute and said, "Ok, go. Will you be able to walk to the rest room alone?"

After assuring Vicky that I was stable, I staggered to the loo and took out my weapon in my right hand, the weapon that had brought me closer to Priety, the weapon that let me share some beautiful moments with her, the weapon that waited for her call....my cell phone. I didn't have any of her photos in my phone, she never allowed me to click her photos. But I had her messages. I started reading them one by one.

By that time Vicky had paid the bill and then he walked towards the loo calling out my name. We went out of the bar with hands on each other's shoulders. Truly, I had missed him in the past few weeks. My eyes filled with tears, I thanked him for being there for me in my hard times.

It was already 9 pm and we still hadn't started studying for the next day's exam. Vicky kept trying to convince me to forget Priety. I agreed for his sake, but the truth was that I could never forget her. We talked about friendship, being there for each other and about girls. Vicky came to the conclusion that spending time and energy and of course money on girls was not worth it. That night, I got acquainted with one truth- Alcohol is a great solvent which dissolves all your woes.

Finally, Vicky dropped me home in an acceptable state after attenuating the vodka effect with the help of some coffee. At home, I tried to behave normal, went straight to my bathroom and brushed my teeth. Then, like a good boy, I sat down to study, not giving my parents any clue about the whole issue.

Tomorrow's exam was of Radar. I tried reading the book, but everything felt worthless without Priety in my life. Though it was tough, I started with few chapters, making an effort to pass. Struggling to concentrate, I studied for some 3 hours and then I slept, as the effect of the liquor was invincible.

For the next one week, I was busy with the exams and efforts to call Priety. She rejected my calls and also avoided me in college. I was in a fix when friends would ask me the reason for Priety and me not talking to each other. I tried concentrating on studies and blocking other thoughts from my mind with the help of songs. But in such a situation, every song reminds you of your love. When such a song played, my mind wandered, overwhelmed with her thoughts, and I would just sit there, in a trance like state listening to that song again and again.

1st June 5.00 pm

I let out a sigh of relief as I walked out of the examination hall. My exams had finally got over; the last paper was of DTSP, the toughest subject of our curriculum. The exam hadn't gone well, but I was least concerned about it. I was feeling very depressed because of Priety's thoughts constantly pinching my brain. In the last one week, I tried calling her many time, but her response was unaltered. She was adamant on avoiding me.

I moved out of college quickly, took out my car and went around looking for Priety. I drove around the campus 2-3 times, but couldn't see her. I knew she wouldn't talk to me even if I approached her, but I wanted to catch a glimpse of her. It was going to be a long time before the results were out and I would not be able to see her till then. Avoiding Vicky and Rahul's calls, I headed home and reached by 5.15 pm. I was all alone, sitting in my living room, engulfed in her thoughts. I was feeling utterly helpless. Just then, my phone buzzed, it was a missed call from Vicky. He must have been waiting for me at college; surely he must be angry at me by now. So I thought of calling Vicky and Rahul later when they would have cooled down. But first, I had to freshen up. Throwing away my bag and clothes on my already cluttered bed, I took a leisurely bath, changed my clothes, made tea and maggi for myself and sat down in front of the television, enjoying my tea.

The doorbell rang…buzz…buzzz. I opened the door. There was a pizza deliver boy, rather man at the door with a pizza in his hands. He quickly handed the pizza to me. Out of nowhere, a pizza was thrust in my hands, I was confused.

I asked, "*Oho bhaiyya*, whose pizza is this, I haven't ordered any."

He said, "The order is on the name of Mr.Sinha."

I thought that dad might have ordered it from the office for me.

Me, "Has the payment been made?"

He said, "Yes, yes."

Fumbling with words, he looked worried.

I was about to close the door, but just then a courier man arrived with a letter for dad from some bank. Handing me the letter, he asked me to sign on the confirmation sheet. I was holding the pizza in one hand and the letter in another, so I turned back to keep the pizza and letter on the table. As soon as I turned, I felt someone holding my mouth tightly with his hand. In a minute, my hands and feet were tied and mouth was stuffed with a cloth. I was bewildered, and tried to free myself from their grasp, but couldn't. The courier man and the pizza man were in my house. They threw me on the sofa and went inside. It was a robbery.

I was forcibly made to sit on the sofa when I tried to get up. They quickly walked to my bedroom, went near the cupboard, which I could see through the open door. My suspicion was confirmed, when I saw them opening the locker of the cupboard with a key. Oh shit, they had a master key. I lay there on my sofa, unmoved. They packed the bag that the courier man carried, with money and jewellery of my parents from the locker.

They were busy looting our stuff, when the courier man got a call. He shared some abusive words with the person on call and then spoke to the pizza man "Shit! That moron messed it, he didn't do his job properly. Hurry up!"

They packed the bag in a few minutes. Laughing at me, they were about to leave, when one of them came back and went near the window. Moving the curtain, he looked down towards the entrance and yelled at the other person "Watchman has returned."

Pizza man "What!" He looked tense. "Don't worry, we will be emptying the loot in the box of the bike, the watchman will not be able to know the real issue."

All the while lying there on the sofa, I was trying to make some sense out of all that was happening around me. Suddenly it hit me; this was the moment that could change my life. I had something to tell them, a plan. So I started making frantic gestures, trying to convince them to open my mouth and let me talk.

Courier man came towards me and said, "Don't move. Hey Santosh, what is this *chutiya* trying to say?"

Pizza man, "You idiot, don't call me by my name. I don't know, come here."

I was trying my level best to stop them and ask to remove the cloth stuffed in my mouth. The guy whom the courier man had called by the name 'Santosh' seemed to be calling someone on his mobile. Finally, frustrated he came to me and removed the cloth over my mouth, pointing a knife on my neck.

Me, "Listen, you people won't be spared."

That courage from my side made me feel breathless, as the person pointing the knife pressed it even more "*Kyun be*. What will you do?"

The firm grip by the knife-holder lowered my volume "I am telling for your betterment. My dad is a renowned doctor in this area; he has good contacts with police. They will surely find you within a day. And yes, the watchman is back too, and I had also seen you, it's now impossible for you to save yourself. What Santosh, am I wrong?...but yes, I can save you."

Pizza man, "What nonsense are you talking. What do you want to say?"

"Listen, the amount you just kept in you bag is nothing…nothing as compared to the money kept in my Dad's bank accounts. If you people are interested to get that, I have a plan for that," I said.

The pizza man was surprised to hear that. He laughed at me, considering my words irrelevant "Haha, now you will be robbing yourself."

I was losing the dominance over conversation, so straight away told them the plan "I will not rob myself, but surely my dad. The plan is simple; you people kidnap me, collect the ransom from my father, divide it with me and then leave me. Just think, this is many times more profitable than this robbery."

Their face showed they were thinking about my plan seriously.

Courier man, "*Abey*, your dad has good contacts with police, right? He can find us, even now."

I was trying hard to convince them, "Yes, he has contacts, but he won't use them; he won't risk his son's life. C'mon now, we don't have time."

I didn't give them time for a second thought. Still looking confused, they finally stepped as per my plan. The courier man left before me and pizza man and emptied the bag in the box on the bike kept in the basement. Santosh and I came down in the lift. Luckily, no one saw us. I sat on the front seat and Santosh behind me on the pizza bike, so that, later it can be explained that the Pizza man kidnapped me, holding a gun behind me. Now the task before me was to ride the bike, something I wasn't very good at. That was the reason I struggled starting it, though finally I succeeded after a few kicks. Then, I rode it with a few swaying movements, out of the complex; the desire of money had taught me to ride a bike. Getting through the long stretch of P.Dmello road and riding till Regal theatre was easy. But, after that, the real struggle started. It was heavy traffic, all the time I had to apply the brakes. As a result I couldn't speed at all. By the time we reached Colaba chawl, I became a perfect rider; it was not that tough, I wished I would have tried it the day Priety had asked for a ride on the bike.

I was following Santosh's directions all the time. We rode through many gullies and *kaccha* roads to reach a small old room in a secluded place finally. It was their den. I wonder how these people found such a place in Mumbai. Santosh parked the bike, took out the robbed cash and jewellery, and kept it in another bag. Then, he moved towards the room and opened the lock. Both of us moved in. The place was dirty. It was a room with a small wooden window, which was closed with the help of a metal wire. There was a table in one corner. The only thing working properly in that room was a wall clock, which seemed as if it had not been cleaned for years. However, that didn't matter much, as the first step of my plan had finally got over.

The courier man arrived 10 minutes after us. Both of them were constantly on call with someone, updating their plans progress. Some 20 minutes later, a boy came there. He seemed worried about my presence. I thought he was their boss. The courier man called him by his name.... 'Javed'.

His face seemed familiar to me. I was busy thinking "Wait a minute...I have seen him earlier, couldn't remember exactly where." After emphasizing a bit, I got the answer "Oh my God, he is the same key maker who made a key some weeks back for the same locker at my home. Oh that means, he made a duplicate key."

He looked worried from the very moment he entered inside the room. Looking at him, others got tense too.

I interrupted them quickly and said, "Hey, don't worry. Nothing will happen to you... "

"Just follow my plan, do as I say."

9

ACHANAK MEIN BHAYANAK

God knows, why these guys have brought this lad here. And what is this plan that this idiot has? This is the first time that I've seen a guy who wants to rob his own dad.

I was highly suspicious of him because this was the first time I was directly involved in a plan and if anything went wrong, I would surely go to jail. I looked over to Dinesh and asked, "*Yeh thik nahin hai, Dinesh bhai.* Call Aadesh and ask him our plan of action from here on."

Dinesh replied, "*Baat ho chuki hai.* We will have to go in with his plan. There is no other option. Let's just do what this lad says."

I was worried as the plan seemed to be moving away from its objective. It was only Aadesh, who I thought would be able to find a way out now, so I walked a little away and phoned him, "Aadesh, what's going on? If Sashank is going to plan the robbery, then we are losing the point. This was all done for the girl, in the first place, remember. If Sashank is going to get the money, then the girl will surely stay with him. Then what am I to gain from this?"

Aadesh, "Don't worry man. Just follow the plan for now. You'll get your girl, I promise. And I'm a little busy now. My mom's not well. Will get back to you soon."

Aadesh was the only person whose words were important to me at this point of time. He was my guide. Listening to him, I agreed to go with the new plan.

1st June 11 pm

One of us had to call up Sashank's dad and ask for the ransom. The amount was yet to be decided, so the four of us got together and after a short conversation, came to the decision that the amount would be Rs 50 lakhs. On hearing the amount Sashank looked at us and said, "Ask for 1 crore."

Boy, he really had a bone to pick with his dad. We all were shocked to hear that, but we didn't react to it as it was going to make our pockets heavier.

We were undecided as to who would make the call. Most of the time, the planning and detailing of every job that these guys did was managed by Aadesh. His absence had set off a little bit of panic in the other three. They seemed reluctant to take the responsibility of calling up his dad. Sashank got irritated with their behaviour and after a short argument, Santosh was given the job. Sashank told us to use his phone so that we didn't get caught. He was very sure that his dad wouldn't go to the police and using his number would leave no trace even after the job was done. I was beginning to trust him now.

Aadesh had decided that Anuradha Nagar in Wadala would be a good location for the exchange, so that remained unchanged. It was far enough from both – our den and Samson Apartments. Also, since it was usually crowded, it would be easier to escape just in case something went wrong.

Santosh called the guy's dad and a deal was struck. He told us that Mr. Sinha was scared and was made aware of the threat to his son's life if he went to the cops. Having said that, he let out a big laugh, symbolic of villains in Hindi movies, to which the guy responded with a blank look, coercing Santosh to stop.

Santosh, "1 crore! *Apni toh lottery lag gayi dost*…just in 3 days we will have 1 crore in our pockets….."

- "50 lakhs…not 1 crore. The rest is mine," Sashank intervened.

Santosh looked at him angrily, "What the hell are you talking about?"

Sashank, "That is why I asked you to demand Rs 1 crore. This is my plan and I want my share. Without my involvement, you would not even get the 50 lakhs, so keep your share and shut up."

Santosh took his gun out and pointed it towards Sashank. "How about this, I will shoot you right now and your dad will never know what happened and we will run away with the money."

I rushed towards him to stop him.

Sashank, "Don't act like a fool; you know you will get caught. My dad has enough contacts to put all of you you behind the bars for life."

After a heated argument, it was decided that Sashank's share would be 40 lakhs and the rest would be ours. Still, 10 lakhs was a substantial amount, I wasn't complaining.

It looked as if our lives were about to change. So far the plan had worked perfectly; the thought of Rs 10 lakhs was baffling. It was the first day of our long wait, and we were already in our dreams. All of us were in a good mood and silently dreaming about what they would do with their share.

I could imagine myself dressed stylishly, jeans and all, like Aadesh, sitting on my bike with my love behind me, waiting for the signal to turn green. Everyone around me would be jealous, while I would be busy with my love, not even noticing them. And then when the signal would turn green, she would say sweetly, "C'mon Javed, lets go to a place where there will be only you and me and no one else." That statement reminded me of her voice I heard it at this guy's house when she had called him with affection. There were many questions in my mind for him, but I kept silent for the moment. I recollected Aadesh's confident words and in a second I was back with the belief of getting her, for sure.

Though we were excited about the money, we had to be cautious. So Toya and Dinesh decided to keep an eye on his dad, just in case he squealed to the cops. They told me that he had not gone to the cops, but had visited a couple of banks. Sashank assured us again that his dad would not take a chance, with his son involved.

Over the next two days, Dinesh and Toya were busy keeping an eye on his mom and dad, while Santosh was busy with the arrangements at Anuradha Nagar. I was given the task to look after Sashank. Due to this, we spent a lot of time together. Initially, I was apprehensive but later on I got on with him quite well. He seemed like a decent guy. He didn't look like someone who could rob his own dad just for the sake of money. There must be some reason.

With time, our friendship and mutual faith grew stronger. After all, our aim was the same.

4th June 3 pm

All of us were sitting in the den, discussing the present status of the plan. Santosh gave another call to Mr. Sinha, confirming the timing and location. He had not gone to the cops and we were satisfied with the way the plan was taking shape. But, we were surely missing Aadesh, so I asked Dinesh regarding the health of Aadesh's mother.

Dinesh replied, "She's a little better now."

I said, "Hope she recovers soon."

Suddenly, Dinesh stood up and said, "C'mon brothers, tomorrow we are going to be rich. *Kya* Sashank, ready to go home? *Paisa layega na tera baap?*"

Sashank, "Ya. You only spoke to him."

And then the rest of the guys left, leaving Sashank and I. They said they were leaving to look for any suspicious movement of the police and after that, they had plans to meet some old friend.

Sashank and I spent the afternoon lying on the floor and talking to each other about our lives. I told him about my earlier life, about my days in the orphanage and how I came about to meet *chacha*, and finally the present situation, as I still struggled to make both ends meet on my footpath place. He seemed very interested in my orphanage days and asked me numerous questions about my life in the orphanage.

I told him about Chintu and the time we shared at the orphanage, the bullies and later how it went bankrupt. He listened to that intently; maybe he had never seen any hardships in his life and found my experiences adventurous. I didn't mind though. Further, when I asked him about his life, he told me about his college life, his friends and some funny moments. As per his description, I found his life absolutely perfect. I mean having parents, good education, money to enjoy life, friends to share experiences and what seemed the best, a girl's company…it was adequate for a peaceful life. I wonder why he was doing all this. I avoided asking him too many questions about the girl as he might get suspicious.

It was getting darker outside and we were quite hungry. These guys had not returned and we were so busy with our chatter that we forgot to get something to eat. Sashank suggested that we eat pizza, so he gave me the names of the dish written on a piece of paper. It was some Pizza Hut near the G.P.O in Fort area. He had written '2 Paneer El Rancho, medium size' and 'Cheese garlic bread'. Though a few ketchup sachets were given with pizza, I took a bottle of it from a store, as I thought it would not be enough. It was the first time I was having a pizza and didn't know how to go about it; it looked like some big *paratha* with a thick border and stuffing. Sashank showed me how to eat it. It was a nice spicy meal and I enjoyed it, especially with the tomato ketchup over it. One thing I didn't like was the price. Just to buy a couple of pizza and some bread, I had to spend Rs 500. But no complaints… I could easily afford it in a few days time when I would have the money.

4th June 9.45 pm

It was getting late. Dinesh and the gang had still not returned. I phoned each of them, but none of them responded. I was worried for them. I had a feeling that something wasn't right. So I locked Sashank up and went to Dinesh's usual hangout place – Richardson Mill.

I reached there, passing through Samson apartment and my empty footpath place. As I entered their *adda*, I heard some noise coming from inside. Someone was laughing. I could also hear Dinesh and

Santosh's voices. I moved nearer, and what I saw baffled me. Santosh, Dinesh and Toya were sitting, having beer with another guy. And this guy was none other than the same *chashmish* that Dinesh had murdered a month back in front of my eyes. I couldn't believe what I saw. How could a man come back from the dead? To know the real truth, I tiptoed to the room and tried to listen in to their conversation.

They were totally drunk and talking to each other loudly.

Dinesh "Santosh *yaar*, am feeling great. I had never thought we'll earn so much. And all because of that Javed."

Santosh "Ya, the fucker really thinks that we are his friends. Hey Toya, *woh raat yaad hai*....when we had supposedly murdered Mahesh?"

Toya "Ya, how can I folgeth?"

The same *chashmish* whom they were calling Mahesh said "I really had to act for so long, man. Held my breath till that idiot Javed was convinced that I was dead. But, why didn't you ask him directly to work with you?"

Santosh "Man, that guy's a saint. He would never have agreed to work with us. Hence, we played this whole thing out."

On hearing all this, I felt as if the ground had moved from underneath my feet. These guys were never my friends. They were with me only for the money. I felt like a fool. I had trusted them, but they had betrayed me.

I left the mill and returned to the room in Colaba. It was 11.20 in the night. I did not feel like talking to anyone; I just wanted to be alone. Sashank asked for his phone. He wanted to talk to some friend of his. Before giving him the phone, I formally asked the friend's name.

He replied, "Priety Verma. She's a friend from college. She must be worried about me. You must have seen her, when you had come to make that key in our house, she was there."

For the first time, I got to know, my signal girl's name...Priety Verma. It sounded good. I gave him the phone and went out.

The den was in a secluded place. No one lived around here. It was raining heavily that night. I came out of the den, walking through the dingy path bordered on both sides by shrubs, wobbling on the stones kept there to make a way out of mini ponds and sat on an old bench outside. It was pitch dark and I could hardly see anything in front of me. As I sat there, I realised that life had changed so much for me in the last few days. From being a simple key maker now I was a thief and a kidnapper. I had sacrificed my honesty for money and now it dawned upon me that it had been too high a price to pay. The people whom I had considered to be my friends had made a fool out of me. I had no name, no respect and no one to care for me. What was the point of living such a life, being run over by others all the time? I desperately wanted revenge.

Dinesh and Santosh's voices were still ringing in my ears. I thought of asking Sashank to run and alert the cops. But, both of us needed the money badly and also I had to stay silent for Aadesh, who I believed to be innocent and my true friend, and also for Priety's sake, I had to be passive.

Half an hour later

Dinesh and the rest returned.

Dinesh asked me, "What are you doing here? It's nearly midnight."

The moment he asked me that, we heard a gunshot from the room. We ran towards the room. I could make out the reason for the sound coming from the room with no one except Sashank inside, but I was curious to get in first to know exactly what had happened. With his long legs helping him to leap through the path, Toya got into the room first. He opened the door with a mere push. The other three, including me entered after him one by one. Stepping in, the first thing we saw in the dim light of the bulb was the pool of blood in which we were standing. The blood seemed to be oozing out from a wound in Sashank's head. This turned their faces pale with fear. I wasn't scared, rather I was confused. So I moved towards him. He wasn't breathing, no movement either. He was lying on the floor and had Dinesh's pistol in his hand. He must have taken it from the table. There was a piece of paper held in his other hand. There was something written on it. Initially I couldn't understand what was going on, but later I was happy that this happened.

10

SASHANK
"HAPPY BIRTHDAY TO ME"

"Hey guys don't worry. Nothing will happen to you."

"Just follow my plan, do as I say."

I began to explain my plan in detail as I had envisaged in the last 30 minutes. It was a simple plan if executed properly and I didn't expect anything to go wrong as these guys seemed to be professionals. The others heard me out intently but Javed just stared at me as if in disbelief. I didn't like the look on his face; he was making me feel guilty already.

After I finished, one of them spoke up, "Give us two minutes, we need to consult our partner."

With a resigned look on my face, I sighed and sat back on my chair, I realised that my fate hung upon that phone call. All of them huddled in a corner and the guy who spoke to me called up his partner…or boss, whoever it might be. After much deliberation, they seemed to have reached some conclusion. I tightened up for a moment when one of them pulled out a revolver from under his shirt but he kept it in a drawer on the old table and I heaved a sigh of relief. Beads of sweat had already gathered on my forehead.

They turned towards me and the same guy spoke up, "Our partner agrees to your plan but keep one thing in mind, if it misfires or if we sense any foul play then you shall not live to see another day."

I relaxed a bit, I was counting on these guys support, and there was no question of any foul play, I would be playing with my own life if I thought of double crossing these guys, black- mailing my own parents was enough for me. But Javed still seemed confused and worried about the plan. I didn't want anything to ruin the deal, so I started talking deliberately to divert everyone's attention from Javed. After two minutes, he stormed out of the room.

Now the next step would be to let my parents know about my kidnapping. It needed to be done discreetly to have the desired impact. After a long discussion, they all decided the ransom money to be of 50 lakhs. But I disagreed, 50 lakhs was not going to be enough by any means. Life had given me this one chance and I wasn't going to let a bunch of brainless crooks spoil it.

"Ask for one crore," I said. They all looked at me in disbelief. It was at this moment it dawned upon me that these people might not be professionals after all. They had stumbled upon a jackpot by chance, led towards it by that key maker guy, Javed. But even he didn't seem to be the mastermind; in fact he didn't even look like he belonged to this gang. The brain working behind everything was surely not in that room at that moment, surely it must be the person these guys were calling all the time. Such situations demanded quick thinking which was beyond these half-wits, and I decided to try and manipulate them around as long as the other person was out of the scene. Also, I knew that my dad could easily manage 1 crore, an established doctor in a city like Mumbai has enough earnings per month that would easily put a top corporate executive to shame, just that it goes unnoticed most of the time.

In a few more seconds, I understood that these goons were *fattus* too.

Santosh, "Dinesh, you make the call....tell him that the boy is kidnapped.. And aaa ask...for the money."

Dinesh who by now had stretched himself comfortably over the muddy floor suddenly sat up straight, as if struck by lightning and began to look for something in his mobile, pressing the buttons furiously, tapping his mobile phone, waving it in different directions as if desperately searching for network "Oh *yaar*, my mobile is not working properly *yaar*. I am not catching range...just a minute *haan*..or else you call."

Santosh, "Toya you.." But he halted in his words.

Toya meekly looked upwards as if admiring the roof but silently he was thanking God for the first time for his slippery tongue, he looked as if he was deep in trance, engaged in some heart to heart conversation with God himself. He frequently used his X-ray vision with the opposite sex but this time he had x-rayed the roof and got in touch with his inner self. He regained his composure in a few seconds and looked around, acting surprised, everyone stared.

Dinesh, "What Santosh, if he called *na*, his dad will simply hang up, considering it some mobile network problem."

They were all hesitating to make the call, the way I and my friends use to do to save talk time.

It was hard for me to be patient.

I stubbornly told them, "Make it quick, people. And what 'ask...ask'. You have kidnapped me. You should order for the ransom, not request." Somehow, my words had the desired effect. They stopped fooling around and again huddled together.

Finally, Santosh decided to call my dad for the ransom money of Rs 1 crore. I gave Santosh my mobile to call my dad, as my number would go into the records, if something went wrong and we got caught.

Leaving Toya with me, the rest went outside, to make the call.

After about 10 minutes, they returned to inform me that my dad had agreed for the deal. Santosh was laughing villainously, "1 crore! *Apni toh lottery lag gayi dost*…just in 3 days we will have 1 crore in our pockets…...." he said.

I corrected him by telling him that their share was 50 lakhs, not 1 Crore, the rest was mine. He stopped in his celebrations and walked towards me angrily "What the hell are you talking about??"

We had a heated argument during which he even pointed the gun towards me, but Javed stopped him. I wasn't scared as I knew that he wouldn't pull the trigger. He could never get the money if he killed me. I kept my composure, he cooled down a bit and finally after a lot of bargaining, I settled for 40 lakhs.

The location decided was Anuradha Nagar of Wadala. But, they weren't happy with one thing; my dad had told them that he would need 3-4 days to arrange the entire amount. I knew that he kept his money in different banks at different locations. But, hearing that, the goons here…I mean Dinesh and all, were worried about my dad going to the police. After battling for a long time, I somehow assured them that he wouldn't go to the police as I was his only child and they would be safe. The goons still didn't have faith in me, that's why they confirmed it by keeping an eye on my father during those days. In a way, waiting for 3-4 days was a good idea. That would surely gain me Priety's sympathy. That was important.

It was tough spending time at this creepy place with no mobile, no television, no computer. But as days passed, Javed and I talked to each other for most of the time. Time moved fast as we enjoyed knowing each other's lives, which were as dissimilar as chalk and cheese. He was born in a local orphanage. It reminded me of something, so I went on asking him more about life in an orphanage. After talking to him for a while, I felt a likeness towards him; both of us yearned to be free from our shackles, and achieve our destiny and also there was something else. I decided to help him. Further he said that he stayed on the footpath, making keys and earning his livelihood. No parents, no girlfriend and no studies too.

My first impression about him was right; he was not a crook at all. In fact, he was a devout Muslim, a godfearing man who could never cause anyone any harm. He was working with these people for a reason I could not fathom, he seemed very hesitant talking to me about it and I didn't press him too much; some things are best kept to oneself, even I could not talk freely about Priety and my earlier life to anyone except the best of my friends, and here I was a complete stranger. Why would he tell me? I liked one thing though, he was not dependent on anyone, for better or for worse. He had only himself to blame. Under normal circumstances that would not seem to be an enviable situation to be in, but to me, it was what I had yearned for all my life, freedom. His life was a struggle; I envied him. He actually started living his life after getting into wrong deeds. That was going to be true on my part too.

4th June 9.45 pm

I was getting bored sitting alone, as Javed, after getting fed up of calling his partners, went to look for them. To fritter away time, I had no option than to have a look at the room. It was too dirty with just the table kept in one corner. There was a wall clock that showed the time, 9.45 pm that meant it was working. It reminded me of one more thing that after 2 hours 15 minutes, was my birthday. It was going to be my best birthday till date, as I was about to get the money till tomorrow evening. And after that, I had planned to run away with Priety and the money to settle somewhere.....away from this world full of villains, especially my dad, who tried to separate me from my love in every way; I think, because he had failed in his love life. Also, the issue of Priety hating me would be solved, with the money.

I walked to the table. It needed serious repairing...sorry; replacement would be a better option. The wooden desk was made porous by the hungry termites. The iron framework was totally rusted. Checking out further, I saw that it had three drawers. Opening with great effort, I saw that the 1st drawer was empty. The 2nd drawer was empty too. Only the 3rd drawer remained, and I wasn't even looking forward to opening it. But, looking back at the time and the empty room, I felt there was nothing to pass the time. So, I opened the 3rd drawer and I was shocked to see what lay inside. It was a pistol and some bullets. It must be the one Santosh had removed from the back pocket of his trousers, I recalled. I don't know much about weapons, but it was surely in working condition, otherwise why would he carry it around. I pressed the trigger a few times aiming at the farthest wall. It was the first time I had looked at a gun so closely, leaved alone holding it in my very hands. After exploring it for a few more minutes, I kept the bullets and pistol back in the drawer.

To divert my mind from these dangerous things I returned to my place, thinking about the coming perks. "Hff...Priety, my love, just see what I have gone through to make it happen, to realize my dream, to have you in my life. Hope you would have got the news." Alone in there I was mumbling to myself, it made me feel that she might be sad about me being kidnapped. And when I met her, she will be there, in my arms.

That night 11.30 pm

Javed came back. He looked dejected. I had no clue as to what had happened. Maybe he was just tired. I requested him to give my mobile to me, to call Priety. I planned to call Priety and tell her that I would be freed from the kidnappers the next day and with a number of requests, the kidnappers had allowed me to make a phone call to her, as she might be worried; that might gain sympathy.

Javed asked me about the person whom I would call. I told him the truth after which he gave me the mobile and went out. I don't know why, but he looked sad.

Dragging himself heavily, he opened the door. It was raining heavily outside. It had been, for the past one and half hours.

I wanted to ask him the reason for his sadness, "Javed..Javed, wait."

But the clamour of the incessant rain was so loud that he hardly heard my voice.

He went outside closing the door with a bang.

Turning back, I switched on my cell phone and called Priety. I was ready with the made-up innocent voice, so that she wouldn't have a clue that I wasn't actually kidnapped.

She received my call in third attempt "Hello Priety. Don't hang up please, listen to me. I have arranged for everything Preity, now nobody can separate us. I will be freed tomorrow. Priety, these kidnappers allowed me to make only one call. Priety I...I.."

Priety, "Sashank. Are you nuts??. Don't you understand what I have already told you. I am least interested in your life. It doesn't matter to me, whether you are at home or kidnapped or alive or dead. As I said earlier, I want you to keep this in your brain forever that I am not at all interested in you. I don't want to talk to you anymore. You are nothing for me. You don't play any part in my life. And for your kind information, I am in a serious relationship with someone. I have a boyfriend, who will be my husband soon. So, please stop disturbing me and please don't ever call or message me. Or else I will complain about you to the police. Ok. Did you get it?"

She cut the call saying these words. She didn't even allow me to speak. She hated me. I felt that my life was worthless. I was sitting there, planning such a huge con job at my own house for a girl who had just thrown me out of her life. I had bluffed my parents for her. I lied to my friends for her. I left everything for her, and she was telling me to forget her. How was that possible?

The whole world started spinning around me. I felt guilty for everything in my life. Without reconsideration, I stood up and went towards the table, opened the 3rd drawer and took out the pistol and bullets, loaded the bullets in the pistol.

"I don't have the right to live after such inhuman deeds. Also, Priety is my life. I love Priety. I wanted to spend my whole life with her. When she has thrown me out of her life, there is no sense to live now."

I took the note out of my wallet. Reading it, I felt like crying. I felt the emptiness of Priety around me. With much effort, I kept the end of the gun barrel on my head. It horripilated me, making my arms weak and my receptors hyperactive. I was sweating heavily. I closed my eyes. The memories of Priety, Javed, Dad, Mom, goons, Friends flashed before my eyes, in a second. To distance myself from these obstacles and to make my decision firmer, I opened my eyes and read the note for last time "To Sashank Sinha. With lots of love and luck. P. Verma. 5th may 2011."

Holding that note, I saw the clock, time was 12.02 am. I wished myself "Happy birthday to me" and then screamed aloud to gain the courage.....Aaarrgghh.

11

"AJEEB DASTAN HAI YEH"

5th June 12:05 am

The scene looked really scary. Sashank lay on the floor, a blackish red pool of blood had formed on the ground around his head. He had Santosh's revolver in his right hand, his finger still on the trigger.

Everyone was shocked.

"Fuck.. What the hell happened? How could he kill himself? Everything was going perfectly wasn't it? Then why.." Santosh was at a loss of words.

I shrugged, "I don't know, he looked fine when I left him here, in fact he was pretty excited about the money."

Dinesh approached the body warily and was about to pick up his gun when I stopped him "I wouldn't do that if I were you, the gun is the only evidence that points towards his suicide if this becomes a police case, leave it there."

Dinesh, "But.."

"It's not as if you have a licence for it anyways, so don't bother. Think what are we going to tell his parents now? I am sure they will inform the police if they don't hear from us".

Dinesh "Fuck that… what are we going to do now.. we'll have to hide somewhere.."

"We should just leave him here, I wouldn't want to touch him, this place is secluded enough, lets just move out," I suggested.

Santosh "You're right, its time to leave Mumbai guys, this is going to be a high profile case, the media will be all over it once the news breaks out".

"Yeth, I aglee," Toya spoke for the first time.

They were ready with their back up plans in a few minutes, Santosh would go back to his village Mau, Toya had a wife in Chennai that no one knew about till now, so he would go there, Dinesh to Nagpur, his hometown. We had alerted Aadesh on the phone, he must have run too.

But I had nowhere to go other than my old footpath corner and I was happy to go there now, but first, we had to split the money.

Dinesh seemed reluctant.

"Your job was to watch over him, why the fuck did you leave him alone?? And now you want your share.." he thundered.

"Don't you blame me! So it was my job now, and you think I can't make out that you guys have been out drinking all the time? You could have stayed here if you wanted, I hadn't asked for this job, and really, this money is from the robbery for which I had made the key, so you might as well shut up".

Dinesh sprang towards me but Santosh stopped him midway, "He's right; we will have to give him his share. It's not the time to fight now. But Javed you need to stay away from the police.."

"I will, I'm not a fool" I spoke, still keeping my angry composure, it was working.

Everyone escaped the same night. I came back to my street, trying to make sense of my thoughts, when Chhamiyaan came to me. He started rubbing his face over my hands, as if he wanted me to cuddle him. When I didn't do that, he came over my lap and sat, getting close. I felt as if he was trying to convey that he had been missing me. It had been almost a week since I had been with him, as I was busy being a puppet for this outside inhuman world. Finally, he slept after some time. I think he was expecting some biscuits, but I did not have any. I actually forgot to get some for him. Even after not caring for him for so many days and forgetting his biscuits, he still felt the same affection for me. Dogs are more faithful than human beings.

Their love is truly unconditional, unlike human. My eyes were feeling droopy.

It was a chilly night and my place was wet too, that's why I wasn't able to sleep. The milk tankers and garbage trucks occupied the road. It was the time when the night dwellers come out for their work, some willingly and some unwillingly. A drug addict was lying in the garbage heap intoxicated, while in the same heap, a rag picker was trying to find something he could sell. A prostitute was walking hastily abusing a taxi driver who was making lewd comments and trying to get her to go with him. A short old man with a white overgrown beard wearing torn clothes and carrying an empty sack was abusing every other person passing by, probably to express his frustration in life. A doctor in a white apron was assuring his teacher on phone that he would bring him cigarettes, for sure. When I tried to analyse their behaviour, the common factor that I found associated was….money. Someway or the other, the desire for money made them do what they did. Even Sashank wanted the money, money that was his but he never had it. Then I thought I needed a good sleep to be fresh at work next day. So in spite of feeling crushed, I somehow managed to go to sleep.

6th June 10 am

I woke up late, still coping with the headache I had due to last night's incident. To get fresh for work, I had a quick bath and went to the mosque after many days. In all this mess, I had forgotten *Allah* all these days. After my prayers, I went down to my stall with a feeling to get money.

With the advent of monsoon, the weather had changed totally that too in just two days. From a hot sunny day, it had turned to a serene breezy day, with a slight yellow tint all over. Happy faces everywhere, enjoying the lovely weather. They remind me of Priety.... the only reason that used to make me happy. Exploring further, I saw a man at his apartment window, in the building just opposite to my stall. He looked happy, feeling the cool air and enjoying a hot cup of tea, as he blew over it before each sip. I was happy too, feeling the same breeze. Really, *Allah* is great, he is never partial. Be the person rich like the one standing at the window or poor like me, he never gets partial to anyone. He showers his assets…his breeze, his rain..to everyone being unbiased. Doing all this, he never asks anything in return. Whereas human…Never does anything without any profit, even loves with some intention. People say that the barter system is only in the history books, but it isn't true. Rather, it is the most prevalent system till now. Everything has got an exchange value, even love.

The very next moment I understood the reason for this human behaviour. It brought a smile on my face. It was not the fault of race, the fact is that no human being can be God.

So with that smile and enthusiasm, I worked till evening. I bought myself dinner with my earnings; it tasted great. After all, I had worked hard for it. I still had the 2 lakhs in my bag, but didn't use them. Looking at the money, made me remember those bastards. By the way, the schedule for the rest of the day was fixed, to live only on hard work.

To have lunch, I went to Kalbadevi. Walking by watching the stores of artistic materials, clothes and wigs, my eyes got stuck to a face mask. It was an oval mask, black in colour with margins of eyes and mouth red. It was a smiling face mask with slanted eyes, displaying wickedness. When I wore it and saw myself in the mirror, I felt it was perfect for me. I mean…it fitted my face. I liked it and I bought it.

One month later

Life was better. I worked so hard, that I did not realize how time had flown. I had not seen anyone for many days. I guess the rest of the guys had not returned to Mumbai yet. It's better they stayed away from me. It was 4:10 pm. I moved out my store and went to my usual signal. I had not seen Preity for many days. My eyes were searching for her, but Sashank too flooded my thoughts.

It was drizzling. A radio was on in a *chai tapri* nearby, playing some old melodies. A traffic policeman was directing the traffic. A part of the road was flooded. People walked around with umbrellas. Some were getting drenched and some drinking tea by the roadside stall. Some were feeling the raindrops by extending their hand out of the car window, while others were busy making plastic tents to prevent their roadside bed from rain. Some were enjoying the monsoon with their lovers, while some just looked disgruntled with life.

The signal was green, but still the bikers and drivers were honking, as it was a total jam created by a taxi driver having a fight with a rich person, because his taxi was hit by rich person's car. The traffic was too heavy to let the bikers get their way. And then I saw her. Priety, in light blue top and blue jeans. But she wasn't on her scooty this time. Instead she was sitting on a bike behind another guy. They seemed glued to each other. The guy, in blue jeans and black shirt had a helmet on, and I couldn't see his face. I wanted to know who this chap was.

Everyone at the *chai tapri* was laughing and making fun of the whole chaos there. It brought laughter to some passive observers. And then, I think to listen to the comment, the chap with Priety removed his helmet. I was shocked to see him, as the chap was none other than….Aadesh. I couldn't believe it….I mean how could Aadesh? I never expected him to be at this place, the place next to Priety. I rubbed my eyes and pinched myself to confirm if it was a hallucination. But, it wasn't. It was the real truth. I swear, God has taken an oath to bewilder me at every moment of my life. But, when I summed up all the past experiences together, I got a clear picture of the master plan that the goons played on me and all my questions were instantly answered.

Aadesh was busy talking with that shrew seated behind him. While he turned back to speak, he noticed me watching him. He looked amazed, just for a second after which he smiled at me, displaying his pride of getting Priety.

At the very moment, a song played on the radio nearby, *"Ajeeb dastaan hai yeh, kahan shuru kahan khatam. Yeh manzilay hai kaunsi. Na woh samajh sake na hum."*

12
MONEY SPEAKS

Aadesh was smiling at me, actually laughing at me. I was cursing myself for trusting him. I knew about their trap, but still I kept on believing that Aadesh was innocent. He was the only one who guided me, luring me with that beautiful bait. Now I knew why.

I looked at him with an enraged look in return to make him feel his guilt, but he was unaffected, with that smile getting even more wicked. Fucking con man. He kept chatting with Priety, acting sweet. Suddenly, the people who were till now standing still, busy watching the free *tamasha* at signal started moving as the show at the signal ended without any winner. So the traffic eased out and when I turned back to see Aadesh, he was gone.

I sat there on my rocky throne feeling the grief of being betrayed.

It was hard to digest the fact that even Aadesh had deceived me. In these times, it's a crime to trust anyone. Aadesh and his friends had betrayed me, Priety betrayed Sashank, and Sashank, the poor dude's gone because of all of this. He had become a good friend of mine.

Evening 6 pm

After my evening *namaaz*, I was going to a place in Grant Road where a building was being constructed. The builder wanted some 50 latch locks for doing the basic furnishing of rooms. He had called me for that. It was going to be a crucial order. Getting such a big deal, that too at a construction site in this hot spot would open doors for me to get orders from other builders too. I was ready with my quotation, setting the price with a bit lower profit, as it would increase my chances. I was walking past the J.J flyover, where I saw Aadesh coming up to me on his bike.

He said, "Hey Javed, I need to talk to you."

I replied, "What are you here for now? You've already killed Sashank. *Ab aur kya chahiye…*"

His face looked worried on hearing that, watching around to see if anybody heard that "Keep your voice low. And look Javed, I didn't do anything on purpose. I didn't kill him. He committed suicide. Look, let's forget everything and become friends."

I felt like killing him then and there. How could a person ask to be a friend to someone after backstabbing him? Forget about asking, how one could even look at him in the face, that too looking so innocent.

I answered, "What do you know about friendship? The word doesn't sound good, coming from your lips."

Aadesh, "*Aisa nahin hai yaar.*"

- "Anyways, I am busy now; if you really wanna know what friendship is, meet me behind Richardson Mill tonight."

"Ya sure, my friend." Aadesh agreed and went away on his bike.

I had planned something for Aadesh, but before thinking about that, I completed the construction deal, which finally went in my favour. While coming back I made an important call. After a few rings, the person whom I had called picked up the call. I notified him, "Aadesh is going to meet me tonight at ten in Richardson Mill. Ok bye."

Night 10 pm

I reached Richardson Mill a bit earlier as I was impatient to meet Aadesh. I had a lot to say to him. I had been quiet for very long. This place has many memories for me, memories of incidents that will be there with me forever. Tonight, a new chapter was going to be added in this list.

Aadesh arrived 10 minutes later. The smugness hadn't left his face still.

Aadesh, "So Javed, what's up? Why are we here?"

I knew everything about the plan Aadesh and his friends used to trap me but I wanted to know the whole truth in his words.

I replied, "You are a two faced dog, Aadesh. Tell me, why did you con me and make me join your gang?"

Aadesh, "Oh, so you finally found out that we were using you….good. Okay Javed, today I'll tell you the truth, believe me this time..the truth. We wanted you to do the key job for us, as it would make our work easier, I chose you because you were this inexperienced helpless chap who could easily be misguided. Initially you resisted, but you had to give in when I brought the girl into the equation. So, we, sorry.. I.. planned the fake murder at Richardson, and it worked out in our favour, getting you emotionally involved in our gang. Look Javed, even you were benefitted by all this. But, yes …."

He was talking proudly about his wicked plans, however I was more eager to know about something else…., that's why I interrupted him to ask "Aadesh, why did you……I mean why Priety?"

He laughed and said, "Calm down, I am coming on that point too. *Sabar karo*…and please don't break my flow. With you doing the duplicate job, everything was going on well." He suddenly became silent, making a sad face, though that too was fake, and then continued, "And then you committed the biggest mistake of your life, you showed me....Miss. Prietty Vermaaaa...I was crazy about that girl, ever since you showed her to me at that signal. I had to make her mine. *Saali, ladki cheez hi aisi hoti hai.* Then you told me about her relationship with Sashank, the first block in my way. I had to get him out of the way, but I also needed his money. I was thinking...thinking..thinking, and then I thought that to open any lock, one needs the key, and there is no better option than a key-maker to have it. So my search ended with you, my key maker. I came up with a plan. I poisoned you against him and got the duplicate out of you. You were never a block in my way; rather you were my stepping stone to success. You were a fool, Javed. How could you even think that you could get a girl like that? Haha...and I think you know what happened later. Anyway, I'll be marrying her in a few days. I have a good job and a great girl. Life's great!"

I felt like strangling him then and there. But, I controlled myself and said to him, "Aadesh, great plan. I appreciate your intelligence. Not only me, but someone else also wants to appreciate you...look behind you."

Aadesh turned around. His face turned white with shock. Sashank was standing behind him with a grin on his face. Aadesh fumbled around for words, "Sa-Sashank!! I thought you were dead!"

Sashank and I started laughing.

I said, "Haven't you figured it out yet, Aadesh? We conned you,

you fool!"

Sashank suddenly stopped laughing. He wasn't grinning any more. There was anger on his face, he lunged at Aadesh and punched him. He also added a few kicks for good measure. After enjoying the view for some time, I somehow managed to stop him and dragged him away from Aadesh.

Aadesh was still dazed. I decided to clear the mystery at last.

I turned towards him, "You must still be shocked at seeing Sashank alive. Well, you should be. But, don't worry, all your queries will be answered; I'll tell you everything. On the 4th of June, when we were in the den at Colaba, Dinesh and the gang left me with Sashank and came to Richardson Mill. When they didn't return for a long time, I was worried and went to look for them. On reaching there, I discovered the truth. The truth that you guys had fooled me. I returned to the den, dejected. Sashank asked for his phone, so I gave it to him and sat outside. After a while, I heard him shout. I ran inside, only to see Sashank with a gun to his head. I snatched the gun from his hand, and asked him what had happened. He told me that Priety was going to marry someone else. I somehow consoled him and told him about my experience at the Mill. As we sat there consoling each other, a plan started shaping in my head. I convinced Sashank to play out his suicide for Dinesh and the gang.

When Dinesh and the others returned, I was sitting outside. At the same moment, Sashank fired a bullet in the room. Listening to that, we all hurried to the room. Sashank did as he was told, he covered his face with the ketch-up and grease mixture, looking as if it was blood, and lay on the floor appearing to be dead. I checked his pulse and breath, and proclaimed him dead. Finally, all of them ran away."

Interrupting me to save our skins, Sashank took over, "On the next day, I went home and told my dad, that I had escaped somehow. Aadesh, I don't have a problem with you. My only regret is that I fell in love with a girl like Priety."

Aadesh had recovered by now. The smug look was back. He started clapping.

He said, "Good plan. But what's the use? I got the girl. You have no evidence against me with regards to the theft."

It was impossible for me to control my anger. "If I want, I can name every one of you to the cops. I know where everyone is right now. A couple of slaps, and your name will be out."

Aadesh looked scared. I liked doing that, but as per Sashank's plan I continued, "Don't worry, I won't do it."

It was Sashank's idea to reveal everything. He knew that, it would be better to tell Aadesh everything upfront, in case he saw him alive later.

The three of us stood there at the mill after the revealing

conversation, silently looking at each other. I was thinking about what had happened in my life: where I was and where I had reached. How wrong I was in judging people and how wrong in choosing love.

Finally, Aadesh made a move to walk to his bike and leave, without saying a word as we had silently agreed to forget the past. We too started to leave, but one thing was still puzzling me. When Sashank had decided to tell Aadesh the truth, why did he lie to him? The truth was that, the day after Sashank's attempted suicide, his dad came to Anuradha Nagar, with the ransom money. Sashank had told me to pose as the kidnapper. I wore a mask, collected the ransom, and handed over Sashank to his dad. The next day, he and his family left the country to keep up the ruse of his death. It was Sashank's plan, as he convinced his family that it would keep them safe. When he returned later, I met him and we divided our spoils.

After we left Richardson Mill, I asked Sashank as to why he had lied.

He said, "Look Javed, if Aadesh comes to know about the ransom money, his devious mind will definitely start working again and hatch a plan to get it. Let him be happy with the girl. It's in the best interest of both of us, if he doesn't know about it."

Sashank and I were happy with the cash. I couldn't believe that someone could be so good to me that he would share half of his money with me. In this world of disguised enemies, it's hard to find a true friend, but I finally got one...Sashank Sinha.

Overwhelmed by his favours, I asked, "Why did you share the money with me, when you knew that I was the main culprit, I had made the duplicate key for your locker?"

Sashank put a hand on my shoulders and said, "*Thik hai na* Javed. We have always been sharing stuff.....”

I was a little confused on hearing that, it was true that we had liked the same girl and we were sharing the money.

- "What do you mean? Are you talking about Priety?"

Sashank "*Nai yaar, kya tu bhi, ladki yaad hai...dost yaad nahin...* Don't you remember chintu, your childhood friend? Well, *chintu ab bada ho gaya hai.*"

- "*aur.....?*"

Sashank "*Aur ab uska naam Sashank hai.*"

Listening to that, I was so happy that I was unable to control my tears. Sashank felt the same, I could make out by his wet eyes. We hugged each other, as long lost friends.

Afterwards, I asked him the reason for not telling me this earlier.

He said, "Javed, if I had told you about myself at the Colaba *adda* that day, you would not have believed me and suspect some foul play. That is why, I waited for today to let you know that."

I hugged him again and we left the place. It was true that neither of us got Priety, but actually she was not worth it.

One month later

Today, I own a small locksmith shop on Mohammed Ali road. It's doing great business. Life is going great. I still see Priety sometimes. But, it doesn't make a difference anymore. Instead I now have three good friends in my life...Sashank, Vicky and Rahul. We meet at weekends to share some happy moments and for some bird watching too. Sashank and I still talk about the incident that changed our lives, but never in front of anyone else, not even Rahul and Vicky.

They all have passed their engineering exams and are working towards opening a computer software solutions company; Sashank's share will be put to good use in the project. He has finally found the love of his life, Duaa. She is a doctor, he told me that they had first met on some train journey and later he found her on facebook. What a love story! I wish I had one like that. I coaxed Sashank into opening a facebook account for me. He also taught me a little about computers. So now I am "online" on facebook all the time and I also make random train journeys every now and then. Life is good.

Initially, Sashank was not ready to return to his parents and thinking of going away from Mumbai, but with great effort I convinced him that though he had a grudge against his parents, they had always been there for him and they had even paid so much money to save his life. It meant that he was important to them; different people have different ways of showing their love. Now, Sashank lives with them and makes an effort to understand their love. They look like a happy family now.

He plans to settle down with Duaa once his software business gets established. He was busy for the last few weeks writing something and now he is planning to release a book, titled.... 'Here sat a key maker...'

Kamina saala.

ABOUT THE AUTHOR

Dr.Makarand S Lohire is a bachelor of medicine and surgery. Born in 1987, he grew up in Ambernath, an industrial suburb of Mumbai. Having recently completed his medical education from the famous Grant medical college, better known as J.J Hospital, he currently works as a medical officer in a government primary health center near Kalyan. The humour and pathos in his writings are a product of the five and half years spent at J.J, observing all kinds of people at the hospital as well as outside, in Mumbai city, the microcosm of India. He has scripted a few short films in his college days and also acted in a few. Apart from his work, his interests are writing fiction, music, cricket and spending time with his pets.

Written a few short stories

1. Fear of love (http://blog.pothi.com/2012/02/14/top-5-in-lknb-

fear-of-love-by-makarand-lohire/)

2. Don't ever breed the greed (http://yourstoryclub.com/short-stories-social-moral/suspense-short-story-dont-breed-greed/)

3. Wit – ness (http://yourstoryclub.com/short-stories-suspense-thriller/short-story-suspense-wit-ness/)

4. Weeping glasses (http://yourstoryclub.com/short-stories-family/short-story-remorse-weeping-glasses/)